Europa World Noir
2013 releases

February	*I Will Have Vengeance* by Maurizio de Giovanni *The Rage* by Gene Kerrigan *The Marseilles Trilogy* (*Total Chaos, Chourmo, Solea*) by Jean Claude Izzo
May	*Blood Curse* by Maurizio de Giovanni *At the End of a Dull Day* by Massimo Carlotto *Garlic, Mint, & Sweet* Basil by Jean-Claude Izzo *Minotaur* by Benjamin Tammuz
June	*A Dark Redemption* by Stav Sherez *The Complete De Luca Trilogy* by Carlo Lucarelli
July	*The Crocodile* by Maurizio de Giovanni *Mapuche* by Caryl Férey *Summertime, All the Cats Are Bored* by Philippe Georget
August	*Three, Imperfect Number* by Patrizia Rinaldi
September	*The Midnight Promise* by Zane Lovitt *The Columbian Mule* by Massimo Carlotto
November	*Everyone in their Place* by Maurizio de Giovanni *Dark Times in the City* by Gene Kerrigan

THE EUROPA WORLD NOIR READER

A tribute to international crime fiction

Europa Editions
214 West 29th Street
New York, N.Y. 10001
www.europaeditions.com
info@europaeditions.com

A special thanks to John Sherman
for his invaluable contribution to this reader.

ISBN 978-1-60945-131-8

Book design by Emanuele Ragnisco
www.mekkanografici.com

Prepress by Grafica Punto Print – Rome

Printed in the USA

CONTENTS

Fiction

Preface

By Michael Reynolds

Seven years ago we assembled a small booklet and titled it *Black & Blue: An Introduction to Mediterranean Noir.* At the time, we were preparing to release novels by Jean-Claude Izzo, Massimo Carlotto, and Benjamin Tammuz, and felt like we were on to something big, something that we had to share with American readers; these books were the first exemplars available in English of a kind of writing that utilized the noir genre as a vehicle for getting at the truth behind the news. There was an urgency to them that lent tremendous vitality to our entire publishing project.

Back then, in November 2005, the streets of Paris were ablaze with riots out of the *banlieue*, Europe's most infamous suburban ghettos, situated on the periphery of Europe's most sophisticated capital. For three months, the entire French nation seemed like a powder keg ready to blow, as the violence spread to Toulouse, Lille, Strasbourg, Lyon, and Marseilles. The riots were sparked when three French youths of North African origin, returning from a soccer match, hid behind a transformer at an electrical substation in order to evade a police checkpoint. Two of the boys were electrocuted to death, and the third was seriously injured. Friends and family say the boys had done nothing wrong; they weren't troublemakers, despite having grown up in a neighborhood in which many young men become precisely that.

Those of us who are dismayed that a young person innocent of any crime would run from the police to avoid routine questioning risk appearing blind to the social conditions that give birth to urban unrest and sedated by the good fortune that our birth and social circumstances have afforded us. Yet we are obliged to run that risk because the questions remain: we *are* dismayed, and the answers we sometimes get do no good. What leads to such distrust between the so-called law enforcement agencies and the people they are supposed to be protecting? How is it possible to overcome that distrust?

Seven years hence, *plus ça change, plus c'est la même chose.* The global economy has crashed. Wall Street has been occupied, in New York and in cities far beyond it. Kim Jong Il has died. Osama bin Laden has been killed. The Arab Spring has come and gone. But the view from New York City finds us still wishing there were someone, anyone, who could explain to us the whys and the wherefores of such blistering civil unrest, from the shooting of Trayvon Martin in Florida to the brutal "policing" of Wall Street occupiers by the NYPD. Not glib journalists, hungry for the next story. Not the ubiquitous "experts" who make careers out of color-commentating others' misfortune. Certainly not the politicians.

We wish there were someone to help us really feel the forces at work in situations such as these, someone to explain if and why and how we are implicated in all of this. Someone who would not be satisfied merely to describe, who would be courageous enough to suggest possible solutions to our human dilemmas. Someone who, with tenderness and compassion, with love, and, above all, with authority and authenticity, could shed light on the dark moral corners of our modern world.

By all accounts, Jean-Claude Izzo was this kind of person. His death in 2000 left a hole in the hearts of those who knew and loved him, left his beloved Marseilles in mourning, and left Mediterranean Noir, the literary genre that his work helped to define, without its champion.

Fortunately, Izzo's work endures in his absence. In his novels, short stories, and essays, one thing is clear: Izzo cherishes his personal liberty and he is willing to defend the liberty of others. He is disappointed, repeatedly, by justice systems that seem to have completely lost touch with the ideal of Equality. But what any reader of Izzo cannot ignore is that far more than Equality and Liberty—those two needy and defiant ideals to which we pay constant lip service—Izzo unwaveringly stresses Fraternity.

Fraternité: far more (or far less) than an ideal, far more difficult to codify and define than its revolutionary sisters, near impossible to guarantee. Without Fraternity, however, Liberty and Equality cannot coexist. Without Fraternity we become enemies, full of suspicion or indifference toward The Other; we return to the Jungle, to the state of animals, or worse.

Izzo understood the importance of Fraternity for our contemporary heterogeneous societies:

> It was good to be in Hassan's bar. There were no barriers of age, sex, skin color, or class among the regulars. We were all friends. Whoever came there to drink a *pastis* sure as hell didn't vote for the *Front National*. And they never had, not once, not like some others I knew . . . Friendship mixed with the smell of anisette and filled the place.

This Fraternity, or "solidarity," to use the word Izzo himself preferred for what he (or his fictional stand-in, Fabio Montale) found in Hassan's bar, was his truth. A truth hard won but for that very reason, solid and sure.

In this *World Noir Reader* we have gathered a number of short articles, essays, and tributes dealing with the topic of international crime fiction in the hope that these writings will bring readers closer to the many important authors whose works have shaped the genre, or are in process of doing so—

Massimo Carlotto, Andrea Camilleri, Andrey Kurkov, Carlo Lucarelli, Ian Rankin, Jean-Patrick Manchette, Maurizio Braucci, Yasmina Khadra, Andreu Martín, Henning Mankell, Petros Markaris, and many others. These authors have a great deal to offer readers from places beyond their respective cities and nations—of this we are certain.

The "literature of truth" championed by Izzo is carried toward by authors across the globe, each writing crime fiction that traffics in human virtue, that sheds a redemptive light on the few small gears that turn for good, not evil. These authors have not forgotten their forebears. The rich, vibrant colors of Jean-Claude Izzo's Marseilles still shine brightly in their prose.

Crime exists. It exists here. It exists everywhere. World noir confronts broad, global themes through an investigation of international crime in its local manifestations. It does so without ignoring real lives—the individual, the human. We are still inside Hassan's bar. Outside, the streets, and people's tempers, are on fire. Outside, someone or something we hardly recognize has taken control of the city. Outside . . . But that is outside. Inside, there is a *pastis* waiting for us, there is a fight breaking out in the corner that will be resolved to the satisfaction of everyone involved with a round of drinks on the house, and Jean-Claude Izzo is leaning against the bar with a cigarette hanging from his mouth and an ever-attentive look in his eyes.

We hope you find our *Europa World Noir Reader*, which we dedicate to the memory of Jean-Claude Izzo, as informative as it is provocative.

New York
October 2012

Michael Reynolds
Editor in chief, Europa Editions

U.S.A.
Matthew F. Jones
Joel Stone

U.K.
Stav Sherez

IRELAND
Gene Kerrigan

SPAIN
Alicia Giménez-Bartlett

ALGERIA
Amara Lakhous

Essays, Interviews, & Tributes

Towards a History of Mediterranean Noir

By Sandro Ferri

Translated from the Italian
by Michael Reynolds

As Jean-Claude Izzo remarks[1], in the beginning there is the Bible: the first book born on the shores of the Mediterranean, the world's first great anthology of violent crime stories. From the outset, from Cain's murder of his brother Abel, this encyclopedic Book of books makes it clear that the history of this sea and the peoples who live on its shores is a history of violence, fratricide, bloodthirsty sackings, abuses of power, lootings and rape. Crime exists. The reasons for its existence are manifold. They reside deep within the soul of man. The Bible tells us that our story begins with a homicide, is followed by others, and others still . . .

Like Cain's heart, the history of the Mediterranean is black.

Then, there are two further extraordinary Noir anthologies: *The Iliad* and *The Odyssey*. Both are vast and variegated collections of atrocious crimes. *The Iliad* glorifies the Greeks' fierce attack on the Trojans for the control of trade routes. Or, if it is more to the reader's tastes, it sings the epic tale of Greek heroes in their valorous enterprise to vindicate Paris's kidnapping of Helen.

The Odyssey, on the other hand, is principally a travel book whose hero wants nothing more than to return home. But his journey is protracted by an inordinate number of intrigues and murders.

[1] "Le bleu et le noir," in *Le Nouvel Observateur*, March 1998; reprinted in this publication as "The Blue and the Black," translated by Howard Curtis.

Bringing to bear the immense power of universal archetypes, all of the Greek tragedies confirm once more that the history of the Mediterranean, of its people and its gods, of its dynasties and its kings, is written in blood.

In light of this, Sophocles' *Oedipus Rex* may rightly be considered the world's first Noir novel. In a public letter appearing in 1995 in the magazine *Les Temps Modernes*, Patrick Raynal, director of the world's most famous Noir fiction list, Gallimard's *Série Noire*, affirmed precisely this:

> If we can broadly define *noir* writing, *noir* inspiration, as a way of looking at the world, at the dark, opaque, criminal side of the world, shot through with the intense feeling of fatality we carry within us due to the fact that the only thing we know for certain is that we are going to die, then *Oedipus Rex* can indeed be said to be the first *noir* novel.

In a brief essay published in *Le Nouvel Observateur* in 1998, another Frenchman, master of the Mediterranean Noir novel Jean-Claude Izzo, reminds us that Raynal had "the courage, or, in some people's opinion, the impudence," to publish a reinterpretation of *Oedipus Rex* in his *Série Noire*, a reinterpretation that struck a decidedly "hard-boiled" note[2]. Izzo seconds Raynal's choice: "The Mediterranean Noir novel," he writes, "is the fatalistic acceptance of the drama that has been weighing upon us since a man first murdered his brother somewhere on the shores of this sea."

The same elements that characterize these "criminal" interpretations of the classic Greek tragedies, interpretations that put the struggle for power in the foreground, can be found in the novels of the German author Christa Wolf, particularly in

[2] "The Blue and the Black" by Jean-Claude Izzo, translated by Howard Curtis.

her rewritings of the Greek classics *Cassandra* and *Medea*. In these works, Wolf tells us that crime and violence are cornerstones of Mediterranean civilization. Medea and Cassandra "investigate" their situations and their worlds and discover that at the bottom of it all there exist crime and criminals.

The Mediterranean Noir novel, therefore, represents a search for truth in places characterized by fratricidal violence, but also by beauty. While these novels offer us a vision of the dark side, the underbelly of society, their settings are invariably places that are caressed by bright sunshine, by blue skies and clear waters.

After this auspicious début under the influence of noir, a début that gives criminality and crime their due (the Bible, *The Iliad*, the Greek tragedies, etc.), Mediterranean literature turns its back completely on the criminal forces at play in our nations and our neighborhoods. For over two thousand years, there was not a single literary movement that stressed this dark side, that emphasized the violent and tragic nature of Mediterranean life. Likewise, no literary movement developed an interest in "the investigation"—that is, the systematic search for the truth.

The literature of ancient Rome did not take this direction, nor did Arabic literature during its period of splendor (contemporary to Europe's Dark Ages). This investigative slant is entirely absent in the traditions of courtly poetry, the ribaldry of the jester and the knave, and the poised verses of cavalier literatures, both serious and parodic. One need only take Cervantes as an example: despite the vicissitudes of his own life, decidedly tragic and even, one might say, noir-esque (the loss of his hand in the battle of Lepanto, his slavery in Algeria, his experience in prison), Cervantes chooses a high, noble, cavalier genre in which to pen his masterpiece, *Don Quixote*. He recounts a tragic story, but he assumes a tone that is both humorous and ironic.

Likewise, the "investigative tone" is nowhere to be found in French, Italian, Spanish literatures of the 17th and 18th centuries. Even the experience of marginalization, which has always been crime's most faithful bedfellow, gives rise in these centuries to artistic expressions that exult in the comic, bawdy elements of the life of petty thieves, conmen, and everyday tough guys.

There are exceptions, of course: the tragic poetry of Villon dealing with life on the margins of the medieval world; Machiavelli's tale of savagery and the necessary commingling of politics and criminality; naturally, Dante's *Inferno*, a vast gallery of crime and criminals. But these few are the only representatives from the pantheon of great writers who have turned their gaze towards the world of crime, culpability, and violence. Italian noirist Massimo Carlotto also directs our attention to the world of "gentlemen bandits & brigands," from Robin Hood to Till Eulenspiegel. But this is a literature belonging to northern Europe, not to the Mediterranean. And, what is more, the Tragic is not a dominant element.

Finally, in the 19th century, a number of great writers attempt an "investigation" into the social and psychological spaces in which crime is born. But once again, this tends to be a largely northern European phenomenon: Dostoevsky, Dickens, Stevenson, the gothic novel, followed by the first real crime novels, those of Sir Arthur Conan Doyle.

There are a few examples of "crime" novels that cast their gaze in the direction of the Mediterranean. In France, Dumas unveils *The Count of Montecristo*, partially set in Marseilles. Even the great Victor Hugo, who of course remains an essentially romantic and Nordic writer, comments that: "The man who does not reflect lives in blindness. The man who reflects lives in darkness. We have no option but black." In Italy, Francesco Mastriani's *Neapolitan Mysteries* (similar to certain French novels, notably those of Eugene Sue, evincing obvious sociological and socialist tendencies) recounts the world of the Neapolitan criminal underworld, a world populated by the Mafia, by rich robber barons, and by "*strangolatori.*"

But these are tentative, "accidental" steps in the direction of

Noir and the Mediterranean. It is not until the twentieth century that we see a genuine birth (or rebirth) of Mediterranean Noir.

The Mediterranean Noir movement begins to take recognizable form only towards the second half of the twentieth century. A particular brand of police or crime fiction commonly bearing the label Noir is first born in America. The name is French, of course, (in American, it is also called "hard-boiled") but the movement itself does not arrive in France until after the first novels of this new genre have been published in America. Raymond Chandler, James M. Cain, and Dashiell Hammett are at the head of the class. They set about to systematically subvert the canonical mystery tradition à la Agatha Christie. In their novels, there is no policeman, inspector, or constable who neatly solves the case and puts everything back in its proper order. Chaos reigns supreme both before and after the investigation. The outcome of the cases, whether solved or not, has no bearing on the general contextual chaos. The author is painfully aware of the fact that out there, in the real world, abuses of power, injustice and violence are the order of the day.

As many contemporary commentators have noted, this awareness corresponds to the growing awareness of a reality formed and manipulated by rabid capitalism, where the difference between legality and illegality is blurred; a reality composed of enormous metropolises, asphalt jungles, on whose margins live hordes of poverty-stricken, desperate individuals, ready to use whatever means necessary to ensure their survival.

In the 1970s, French author Jean-Patrick Manchette, is the first to articulate the characteristics of the contemporary noir novel. In an article entitled "Black Like France," published in the magazine *Pulp*, Valerio Evangelisti explains Manchette's contribution to the genre:

> Manchette delineates criminality's arrival into the otherwise ordinary arenas of political and economic power

> and describes how, during a period following hard upon a series of failed revolutions, this criminal element starts to impregnate everyday life. Given these changes in the social fabric, the genre we refer to as noir essentially stops being a simple literature of escapism and becomes a penetrating comment on contemporary times, a literature that pulses with actuality, that is stained with blood just like the contemporary world it describes. This change first occurs in the United States (Hammett, McCoy, etc.) and then spreads to the rest of the world. Noir's watchword is pessimism; its weapon is a certain disenchanted honesty. Behind these sentiments lies a kind of moral indignation on the part of writers who once hoped to turn the world upside-down and, having failed, are forced to limit themselves to describing it, in the process pointing out its many contradictions and aberrations.

But we are still dealing with an American and/or northern European literature, inextricably tied to social conditions that are not those of the Mediterranean: sprawling metropolises, rootless peoples with little or no connection to the neighborhoods in which they live, the solitude of grey northern cities, the deterioration of the family.

Several groundbreaking Mediterranean authors begin looking at reality through a noir lens during this same period, and they are under the sway of decidedly different elements: strong family and clan ties, closed communities that are bound to their land and/or neighborhood, minimal urban development. Jean-Claude Izzo considers Albert Camus's *The Outsider* to be the prototype of the contemporary Mediterranean Noir novel. It is no accident that Camus is one of very few writers to have been "uprooted" from his Mediterranean home. He is a *pied-noir*: a French-Algerian *émigré* in France. And in this, he brings (or brings back) to contemporary literature one strong element that has always belonged to this region's tradition, but which seems to have been forgotten: the sensation of being uprooted. This is linked to the intense and continuous migration that characterizes the entire history of *Mare Nostrum*: the "tragic destiny" weighing on individuals, "the world's tender indifference" to the suffering and solitude felt by these individuals, the sporadic explosion of violence to which they are subject.

Leonardo Sciascia is another whose oeuvre represents one of the genuine precursors of the Mediterranean Noir novel. His work is dominated by the search for truth and the portrayal of a society dominated and corroded by organized crime. Many of his books are bona fide mystery novels. He is one of the first authors to give this genre, previously considered "low literature," the cachet of high literature. Unlike Camus, Sciascia writes explicitly about crime, violence, and the mafia. Yet, the criminal milieus he describes appear to have been subject to few of the monumental changes that modernity has brought to this region. In his Sicily, old-fashioned mores dominate; the criminality he writes about has not "evolved." It has been neither uprooted nor contaminated by outside influences.

To find more recent and modernized contributions to the development of a specifically Mediterranean variety of contemporary noir one must look to the literatures of the eastern Mediterranean, to Levantine authors, and to authors from the Middle East, from Egypt and the Balkans. The tragic sense of life is more pronounced in the work of these authors, as is the sense of deracination and of perpetual movement. Like Panait Istrati, born to a Romanian mother and a Greek smuggler father, who was himself reared in an array of cosmopolitan, multiethnic port towns along the shores of the Black Sea. Disembarking, after many adventures, in France and finding there a temporary home and a language in which to write, he expertly renders this fundamental component of Mediterranean life. His settings are characterized by vast migrations and a burgeoning cultural mix, they are places that thrive with human exchange and trade, but also with violence and hatred directed at the Other. His characters are sub-proletarian, mariners and smugglers.

Indeed, in Middle-Eastern writing, this type of milieu and these kinds of characters—ports, travelers, mariners, smugglers—are quite common. In his novels, the Cairo-born Egyptian writer transplanted to Paris in the post-war period, Albert Cossery, recounts the world of marginalization and small-time criminality permeating the Egyptian capital's souks. He draws inspiration from these contexts for a florid philosophy devoted to idleness and deviance. The Israeli novelist, Benjamin Tammuz, a Russian who, as a child, relocated to the shores of the eastern Mediterranean, captures the mystery that cloaks the lives of the peoples who live around this sea and the legacy of ferocity weighing upon them, augmenting the violence that is an abiding characteristic of their histories. These characteristics are particularly pronounced in his most famous novel, *Minotaur*.

In Greece, at least two authors lead the way towards a new kind of Mediterranean Noir novel. In his book *Z*, Vasilis Vasilikos recounts some of the political facets of large-scale crime; and in *The Story of a Vendetta*, Yorgi Yatromanolakis tackles crime's anthropological features, particularly those connected to one of the Mediterranean's oldest and most violent traditions: the feud.

These authors pave the way for the advent of the authentic contemporary Mediterranean Noir novel. The noir novel, as mentioned, from its origins in America, arrives in Europe in the seventies via France. Both the forerunners of this important movement in French—Georges Simenon, Léo Malet, and Boris Vian—and the exponents of the true French noir that began to surface in the seventies—Jean-Patrick Manchette, Didier

Daeninckx, Pierre Siniac, Serge Quadruppani, and many others—recount metropolises (almost exclusively Paris) where capitalism operates at advanced level, metropolises mired in regional social and interethnic clashes. As opposed to their American counterparts, these authors are imbued with an intense political consciousness influenced by the upheavals in 1968. They (or their generation) tried to change the world, and failed. Their vision is characterized by the pessimism that this failure has bred in them. They now see all the world's injustices and its occult powers laid bare, and they cannot remove their gaze from the decay hiding within high-rise buildings, and the desperation of the slums. They carry with them a characteristic sympathy for society's losers, and despite their disappointments in the political and social arenas, they are thirsty for the truth.

But the Mediterranean shoreline is still a long way away. The landscape, or rather the seascape, is missing; the colors and the odors are nowhere to be found. The violence that is born in the grey industrial wastelands of sprawling northern cities, in the dank cold and lingering darkness, is one thing. The shocking, sudden violence of the Mediterranean—violence lying dormant in human limbs caressed by the heat of the sun, and a sea that overwhelms—is quite another. The ferocious passions of the south, its oppressive beauty, the "gilded unhappiness" that Camus speaks of, all are missing. The peoples and ethnicities swarming around the Mediterranean's shores, clambering here from the south, from the east, to claim their share of the riches are nowhere to be seen. There is no blue and black, the two abiding colors of the Mediterranean according to Jean-Claude Izzo.

Perhaps one of the first authors who deliberately wrote Mediterranean Noir novels is the Spaniard Manuel Vázquez Montalbán. At the core of his novels, there is a great Mediterranean port: Barcelona. Food, gastronomy, the pleasure of being seated at a table in good company, the Mediterranean lifestyle, that antique art of living that has reached its apotheosis in this region: these are the elements that dominate his settings. There is also a political dimension, linked to present consequences and their relationship to past conflicts. This same dimension will be rediscovered several years later in authors whose work consolidates the success of Mediterranean Noir: Izzo, Khadra, Martín, Carlotto, and others. In Vázquez Montalbán, however, these characteristics remain embedded in a tone that is, essentially, far from tragic. At times, indeed, it is often openly and intentionally comic. The cloak-and-dagger game of the traditional police novel prevails, and knowledge of real criminality is underdeveloped.

We find the same characteristics in the novels of Andrea Camilleri, where costume, fun and games with the Sicilian dialect, and regional mores and customs count far more than real criminality. Another Italian author, the Neapolitan Peppe Ferrandino, seems to be heading in the same direction: reality is, in some ways, reinvented. The new criminal realities of the Mediterranean and the various conflicts attendant upon them interest Ferrandino only insofar as they provide the catalyst for something different. In and of themselves, they do not represent fertile terrain deserving of deeper inquiry.

This "playful" vein is furthered, in a less dramatic mood, by the Moroccan author Driss Chaibri, and the investigations of his Inspector Ali. With wit and humor, these books introduce us to crime as it unfolds on the southern shores of our sea. Contemporaneously, two original sources of psychological noir come to us from Israel, the blackly humorous novels of Edna Mazya and the more traditional mysteries of Batya Gur, each portraying specific aspects of Israeli society with expertise and panache. Another female writer, Shulamit Lapid, completes this trio of Israeli noir, unique among the literatures of the Mediterranean inasmuch as it is composed of three women. Another author, notable for both her finely honed talent and for the fact that she is a female author writing in a genre that is, in this region, dominated by males, is Elena Ferrante. Her *Troublesome Love* captures the tragedy and the latent violence that are perennial features of an ancient Mediterranean tradition.

But real violence breaks in, hand in hand with the ancient but seemingly forgotten tradition of Mediterranean tragedy, in the novels of the Frenchman Jean-Claude Izzo, the Algerian Yasmina Khadra, the Catalan Andreu Martín, the Greek Petros Markaris, the Italians Massimo Carlotto, Carlo Lucarelli, Giancarlo De Cataldo, Osvaldo Capraro and Maurizio Braucci, and the German-born author based in Trieste, Veit Heinichen. These novels are born in port towns like Algiers, Marseilles, Barcelona and Naples, or in frontier towns on the northern borders of Italy. They share a common understanding: the Mediterranean has become, once more, a region rife with clashes, and political/ethnic conflicts; a place teeming with sackings of various sorts, with the fight for survival, with immense waves of migration, with war, with colossal concentrations of vested interests. Criminal appetites from all over the world—from the Slavic countries, from China and Southeast Asia, from Nigeria and central Africa—converge on the Mediterranean and enter into conflict with local criminal realities—the Sicilian Mafia, the camorra, the criminal milieu of Marseilles and the organized crime rampant in North Africa. Furthermore, this criminality is increasingly linked to "legal" or "respectable" activities, creating an opaque fabric that is virtually impenetrable.

This reality is continuously and contiguously undergoing transformation. It is influenced by new migration patterns and new criminal interests. It is, as Massimo Carlotto has noted, a reality that is determined by the lack of a genuine culture of investigation, and the lack of certain mechanisms that would otherwise ensure the integrity of crime scenes. This means that the solutions to criminal cases rest entirely in the hands of the investigator and his or her ability to manipulate shreds of information supplied by informers, collaborators, and contacts who inhabit a variety of marginal and largely illegal contexts.

Of course, these factors supply an inestimable wealth of incandescent material suitable for literary creation. Ambiguity, the razor's edge between right and wrong, the often slight differences that separate the good guys from the bad guys, characteristics that have been part of noir since its origins in the United States, are further accentuated by factors that are thoroughly Mediterranean.

Invariably, these novels are peopled by indifferent cops (or ex-cops), private investigators, and small-time crooks who are all painfully aware of the ominous growth of political-economic power structures that cohabitate with criminality. They are impotent and inefficient before this overwhelming power. In the final equation, their methods and the means at their disposal amount to naught. These personages are often on the side of the victims of this conglomeration of legal and illegal interests: immigrants, ex-cons, small-time crooks, and losers. Their real objective is not necessarily that of solving the case or finding the guilty party—though this may sometimes be the catalyst for their investigations—but rather to use whatever means necessary, legal or illegal, to protect the weak and to vex the powerful. These novels are set wherever vast movements of people and power happen, wherever there is conflict and massive accumulations of wealth.

The prevailing vision in the novels belonging to the genre known as Mediterranean noir is a pessimistic one. Authors and their literary inventions look upon the cities of the Mediterranean and see places that have been broken, battered, and distorted by crime. There is always a kind of dualism that pervades these works. On one hand, there is the Mediterranean lifestyle—fine wine and fine food, friendship, conviviality, solidarity, blue skies and limpid seas—an art of living brought almost to perfection. On the other hand, violence, corruption, greed, and abuses of power. There is sadness in these books, and a sense of longing for what the Mediterranean could have been: Khadra's Algeria disfigured by violence, corruption and fanaticism; Izzo's Marseilles devoured by the greed of property developers and the racism of the National Front; Carlotto's Italy insulted by a justice system that doesn't work.

The story of this sea is blue and black, and it is still being written . . .

EULOGY FOR JEAN-CLAUDE IZZO

By Massimo Carlotto

Translated from the Italian
by Michael Reynolds

Recalling the work and the person of Jean-Claude Izzo will forever remain painful for those who knew him. Izzo was first and foremost a good person. It was impossible not to feel warmth for that slight man who always had an attentive, curious look in his eyes and a cigarette in his mouth. I met him in 1995, in Chambery, during the Festival du Premier Roman. Izzo was there to present *Total Chaos* (*Total Khéops*). I bought the book because its author stirred my interest: he seemed a little detached in many of those cultural gatherings, as if faintly annoyed by them, as he was most certainly annoyed by the quality of food and wine offered by the organizers. I read his book traveling between Chambery and Turin, where the Salone del Libro was underway. I found it a superb, innovative book, an exemplar in a genre that was finally starting to establish itself here in Italy. I recommended it to my publishers. And not long after Izzo arrived in Italy. A few sporadic meetings later, I went to Marseilles for a conference. Izzo was not there. He was in hospital. Everyone knew how serious his illness was. Marseilles was rooting for its noirist. Every bookshop in town filled its display windows with Izzo's books. Then, on January 26, Jean-Claude left us. He wasn't even fifty-five. He left us with many fond memories and several extraordinary novels that convincingly delineated the current now known as "Mediterranean Noir."

Autodidact, son of immigrant parents, his father a barman from Naples, his mother a Spanish seamstress. After lengthy battles as a left-wing journalist, having already written for film and television, and author of numerous essays, Izzo decided to take a stab at noir, penning his Marseilles Trilogy, *Total Chaos*, *Chourmo* and *Solea*. The protagonist: Fabio Montale; a cop.

Montale, son of immigrant parents, like Izzo, and child of the interethnic mix that is Marseilles, defiantly stakes out his ground in the city that gave birth to the *Front National*.[1] In *Solea*, Izzo writes:

> It was good to be in Hassan's bar. There were no barriers of age, sex, skin color, or class among the regulars. We were all friends. Whoever came there to drink a *pastis* sure as hell didn't vote for the *Front National*. And they never had, not once, not like some others I knew. Here, in this bar, every single one of us knew why we were from Marseilles and not some other place, why we lived in Marseilles and not some other place. Friendship mixed with the smell of anise and filled the place. We communicated our feelings for one another with a single look. A look that took in our fathers' exile. It was reassuring. We had nothing to lose. We had already lost everything.

Izzo's writing is political, in the tradition of the French neo-polar novels[2], and the writing of Jean-Patrick Manchette. But compared with Manchette, who does not believe in direct

[1] The *Front National* (National Front in English; acronym: FN): a far-right reactionary political party in France, often accused of being racist on account of its opposition to immigration. The party was founded in 1972, is still headed by Jean-Marie Le Pen, and is generally considered to be of the far right, although Le Pen denies this qualification.

[2] Neo-polar: the 1970s-80s version of the French mystery novel, after the rebirth of the genre following May '68. Often a politically-oriented novel with a social message.

political action inasmuch as he believes it is ineffective and doomed to failure, and who limits himself to using noir as an instrument with which to read reality, Izzo goes further. His use of the noir genre is not limited simply to description but penetrates deep into the heart of the incongruities, leaving room for sociological reflection and for a return to his generation's collective memory, and above all, gives sense to the present day. Via Montale's inner journey, Izzo declares his inexorable faith in the possibility of transformation, both individual and collective. The point that matters most to Izzo, politically speaking, that is, the point that cannot be abandoned, is the existence of a united culture. From the defeats of yesterday come the losers of today. From this perspective, Montale is an extraordinary figure. Son of marginalization, he joins the police so as to avoid the criminal margins. He abandons his group of childhood friends, a group that embodies multiple ethnic differences, but he will never forget his roots. This becomes a source for his feelings of guilt when faced with his role as cop in a society that is becoming increasingly intolerant. An internal gestation and growth obligates him to leave the police force and to become a loner in search of the justice that is not furnished by the courts. What gets him into trouble is the ethic of solidarity and the desire, common to culturally and ethnically mixed milieus, to find a place and a moment in which he can live peacefully.

On Mediterranean Noir

Solea, the concluding installment in Izzo's Marseilles Trilogy, is flamenco music's backbone, but also a song by Miles Davis. Indeed, music is one of the author's passions. Particularly jazz and the mix of Mediterranean rhythms that characterize contemporary southern European and North

African music. In Izzo's writing, however, music does not simply represent rhythm and a source of nostalgia, but also a key to understanding generational differences. Montale contemplates the merits of rap music. He doesn't like it much, but his reflections represent a kind of understanding as to its intrinsic worth:

> I was floored by what it said. The rightness of the intentions behind it. The quality of the lyrics. They sang incessantly about the their friends' lives, whether at home or at the reform school.

With *Solea*, Jean-Claude Izzo gives substance to the political intuition that is the cornerstone of Mediterranean Noir. He understands that the sticking point the movement must face consists in the epochal revolutions that have transformed criminality. Babette Bellini's investigation1 does not result in the typical affirmation of the Mafia's superiority and organized crime's collusion with higher powers. Izzo defines the outlines of Mediterranean Noir when he introduces into his novel the principal contradiction present in the crime-society dyad: the annual income of transnational criminal organizations worldwide is ten thousand billion USD, a sum equal to the GDP of many single developing countries. The need to launder this mountain of dirty money is at the root of the dizzying increase in the corruption of institutions, of police forces. It is also the catalyst for strategic alliances between entrepreneurs, financial policing bodies, politics, and organized crime. The society in which we live is criminal inasmuch as it produces crime and "anti-crime," resulting in an endless spiral in which legal and illegal economies merge in a single model. Call it, if you will, a socio-economic "locomotive," as in the case of northeast Italy.

Mediterranean Noir, in this sense, departs from the existing conception of French Noir, and likewise from the modern police novel. The novel no longer recounts a single "noir" story in a given place at a given moment but begins with a precise analysis of organized crime.

Another of Izzo's intuitions was his having individuated the Mediterranean as the geographical centre of the universal criminal revolution. There is a rich fabric of alliances in this region between new illegal cultures emerging from the east and from Africa. These alliances are influenced by local realities, which they in turn absorb into themselves. As a result, they possess the means to pursue direct negotiations with established power structures.

This is what Mediterranean Noir means: to tell stories with a wide swath; to recount great transformations; to denounce but at the same time to propose the culture of solidarity as an alternative.

Mediterranean Noir: The Bloody Continental Take on an American Genre

By Dana Kletter

Originally published in the Boston Phoenix[1]

It all starts with murder. Since Dashiell Hammett took the crime story out of the drawing room and into the street, mystery has ceased to be the meat of the story. Hammett used his crime fiction as a magnifying glass to examine capitalism's toll on America. Sometimes he found his perp in that lens, but it was less about whodunit and more about who had the power and money to do what he or she wanted.

Crime fiction in Italy and France today has become as prevalent as it was in the US in Hammett's heyday. The "Mediterranean noir" novel also acts as a lens, trained on European political and social structures. The best of it is making its way to the United States via publishing houses such as Europa Editions and the *New York Review of Books* Classics series.

American noir was peopled with hoods, hard blondes and the rich husbands who owned them, and all the yeggs in yeggdom. Mediterranean noir portrays a Europe where the detritus of postwar, post-Soviet, and post-colonial society drifts across the continent, battling, exploiting, ripping off, and killing one another. Spanish anarchists, Albanian lap dancers, Croatian war criminals, Romanian whores, Moroccan drug dealers—it's not so much that they have a price, it's that they have no place.

Massimo Carlotto's hard-boiled thriller, *The Goodbye Kiss* (Europa, 2006), begins, of course, with murder, specifically a

[1] *Boston Phoenix,* April 27, 2006. Reprinted with the gracious permission of the author and the *Boston Phoenix.*

"double-crossing execution." Pelligrini, a former Italian leftist revolutionary and self-proclaimed "prick filled with delusions of grandeur," has been on the run ever since he killed a man. Sentenced to life in absentia, he makes a run for it—to Central America, where he plays at being a revolutionary. When Pelligrini has had enough of the brutal life of the jungle guerrilla, which makes his militant activities in Milano seem like a game, he decides to return home. He shoots his only friend in the back and heads for Italy. Thus begins Pelligrini's mission to erase his past.

Pelligrini wants to be an ordinary guy—"like everybody else . . . just a face in the crowd"—but he can't untangle himself from the criminal life. Fractured Europe's displaced millions provide him with an endless supply of accomplices. Neo-Nazis, latter-day Leninists, every asshole holding a grudge over the loss of a beloved country that was autonomous for five minutes in the 16th century—Pelligrini uses them all. Each new scenario that holds the promise of bringing him the money he needs to be free comes with a new set of problems. And the only solution he can see is to kill everyone and start again. *The Goodbye Kiss* is not for the squeamish. The body count is high, the nihilism quotient higher.

The novel plays off Carlotto's autobiography. He was a member of the radical left-wing Lotta Continua, the Ongoing Struggle. Implicated in a murder, he was acquitted, then re-arrested and retried. He escaped to South America but eventually came back to Italy to turn himself in. It took 18 years to clear himself, eight of which he spent in prison. Today he is the reigning king of Mediterranean noir; his "Alligator" detective series has made him one of the most popular authors in Italy.

The American noir hero/anti-hero was a wiseacre. He held hard to his Emersonian individualism. He pooh-poohed the idea that he might have any redeeming features. Books and films showed psychological portraits of alienated and ascetic guys who might have been good, if things hadn't gone bad.

They used the language of the street and the poetry of violence, and, in the guise of genre writing, critiqued social corruption ("It is not a fragrant world," Raymond Chandler said) in a way that highbrow literature couldn't seem to.

Hammett and James M. Cain's bleak portraits of modernity spoke not only to Camus and Sartre, but to succeeding generations of writers who have appropriated the form—crime fiction with noir's characteristic dark fatalism—and turned its penetrating gaze on their own societies.

The protagonist of Jean Claude Izzo's *Total Chaos* (Europa; originally published in 1995, and set in the early '90s), Fabio Montale, illustrates the difference between the American- and Mediterranean-noir hero. He values, above all else, loyalty to the friends he grew up with in the projects of Marseilles. Despite the fact that he's a cop and they are criminals, their shared heritage—the children of hard-working Italian and Spanish immigrants fleeing Mussolini and Franco, they "did the jobs the French wouldn't touch"—bound them. A sense of community and a debt of honor draw Montale to the old neighborhood to investigate their murders.

To solve the crime, he must negotiate the street gangs, corrupt cops, and Mafioso of the crumbling projects, and battle the rising neofascist and fundamentalist movements. The chapter headings are a poetic shorthand for Montale's real and existential struggle: "In Which the Most Honorable Thing a Survivor Can Do Is Survive"; "In Which at Moments of Misfortune You Remember You're an Exile."

Izzo, who died in 2000 at the age of 55, scatters his prose with song lyrics, poetry, and fantastic descriptions of the sun-dazzled, sordid city. The austerity of American noir is supplanted by every sensual delight Marseilles has to offer: beautiful women, perfectly grilled sea bream with aioli, copious amounts of rosé and pastis.

The novels of Leonardo Sciascia (1921–1989; pronounced "shasha"), recently released by the *New York Review of Books*

Classics series, are the most elegant of the Mediterranean detective fiction. Sciascia's writing owes more to Pirandello and Calvino than to Hammett or Chandler. Both lyric and ironic, his prose reveals a stratified Sicily, the island's inhabitants embedded and held by each layer of sediment: church, family, political party, and Mafia. All are bound by a code of silence and resigned to the way things are, always have been, and always will be.

In *The Day of the Owl*, one of Sciascia's best books, Bellodi, a "mainlander," as the natives derisively call him, comes south from Parma to serve as captain of the carabinieri. He must solve the broad-daylight murder of a local businessman who resisted the Mafia's demand for protection money. Eyewitnesses will reveal nothing, their faces "as if disinterred from the silence of centuries." The local snitch, whose job is as much to mislead as to enlighten, meets with Bellodi. He gives him misinformation, thinking of "those other informers buried under a thin layer of soil and dried leaves high in folds of the Apennines . . . staking their lives on the razor's edge of a lie between partisans and fascists." He is shot on his own doorstep.

In between chapters, anonymous dialogue—conversations unattributed but understood to be among politicians, Mafioso, and clergy—is a "Greek chorus" singing the party line: there is no Mafia, there is no collusion, outsiders will never understand.

In the showdown between Bellodi and the reigning don, Bellodi does not grasp what he is facing: "Beyond the pale of morality and law, incapable of pity, an unredeemed mass of human energy and loneliness, of instinctive tragic will."

Sciascia wrote fearlessly about Sicilian society in which "'right' had always been suffocated by violence." His true-crime close reading of the kidnap and murder of prime minister Aldo Moro in *The Moro Affair* laid bare the corruption of Italy. In fact, all of his books are haunted by the fascist past, which forever compromises his beloved country's future.

Dark Paradise
By Charles Taylor

Originally published in The Nation[1]

"Marseilles is paradise. They respect me here. I'm not a wog." That's the voice of an Algerian soldier fighting for France in Rachid Bouchareb's 2006 World War II drama *Indigènes* (released here under the terrible title *Days of Glory*). Fifty years after VE Day, the opposite could be spoken by nearly any of the contemporary Arab and Algerian characters in the hard-boiled novels that form Jean-Claude Izzo's Marseilles Trilogy. The Arab youths who endure suspicion and harassment from the cops and the prejudice of the native non-Arab French, who are the target of violence from the far-right National Front and the fool's game of fundamentalist Islam: almost all of these kids feel like wogs.

And yet, as Izzo writes of his native city, Marseilles is a kind of paradise. The three books that make up his trilogy—*Total Chaos*, *Chourmo* and *Solea*—can be read as an extended love letter to the city. Izzo, son of an Italian father who had immigrated there, spent most of his life in the city. His output wasn't vast. It included the trilogy, two novels—*The Lost Sailors* and *A Sun for the Dying* (the latter will be brought out later this year by Europa Editions)—and a book of short stories. He was one of those rare writers lucky enough to be popular with critics as well as the public, though nothing surpassed the popularity of the trilogy, which was written from 1995 to '98. Izzo never got

[1] *The Nation* October 4, 2007. Reprinted with the gracious permission of the author and *The Nation*.

a chance to build on the acclaim and popularity of the books. In 2000 he died of cancer at the age of 55.

In the trilogy, Izzo describes the city as an ever-unfolding flower of sensual delight, a place where natural glory, the sun and the shimmering presence of the Mediterranean exist side by side with the man-made glories of a polyglot city. At times the progress of Izzo's story might be nothing more than the movements of his hero, Fabio Montale, as he drifts from one of the city's pleasures to the next. "There's nothing more pleasant," begins *Chourmo*, "when you have nothing to do, than to have a snack in the morning and sit looking at the sea."

It's a measure of how often paradise is delayed that Fabio almost always has something to do. The Marseilles Trilogy is Fabio's story, and as with all disillusioned idealists, which is to say almost all classic heroes of detective fiction, it's the story of a romantic. Fabio starts out as a cop in *Total Chaos*, the kind who tries to take on the role of good liberal social worker. By the end of the book, in which he investigates the murders of a boyhood friend and a young Algerian girl (whom Fabio has befriended and fallen in love with), this good cop, who has solved the case, is nonetheless so disgusted by the corruption of the force that he quits and restricts himself to his little seaside bungalow, content to fish and spend time with his elderly neighbor, Honorine:

> And one day I woke up and realized I'd lost all my power. I'd been disowned by the anti-crime squad, the narcotics squad, the vice squad, the illegal immigration squad . . . I'd become just a neighborhood cop who didn't get any important cases . . . I wasn't the kind of cop who would shoot a punk in the back to save a colleague's skin, and that meant I was dangerous.

But of course, Fabio keeps getting pulled back in, as much

by his own nature as by the fact that, in each case, a woman he loves needs him. In *Chourmo*, it's Fabio's cousin Gélou, who comes to him when her son disappears. And in *Solea*, I"s Babette, a journalist and occasional lover who effects her own disappearance when a story she's working on causes the Mafia to begin hunting her.

Each of these cases is intimately bound up with Fabio's past, none more so than the murder at the beginning of *Total Chaos*, a death that leaves Fabio the last survivor of a trio that spent their adolescence pulling stickups. He called it quits after a druggist was left paralyzed in one botched job; his buddies didn't.

But the constant evocation of the past in these books serves to highlight the present and the changed city that Fabio loves too much to leave. "Marseilles is a city of exiles," Fabio says in *Chourmo*. "It'll always be the last port of call in the world. Its future belongs to those who arrive. Never to those who leave." The trilogy might be summed up by an argument that Fabio, whose parents were from southern Italy, has with Gélou after she tells him that she and her husband weren't crazy about the fact that her son's girlfriend is Arab. "What were you afraid of?" Fabio harangues her:

> That this Arab girl would stick out like a sore thumb where you live? For fuck's sake, Gélou! Don't you remember what your father was? What they called him? Your father, and mine, and all the nabos? Harbor dogs! That's right! And don't tell me it didn't hurt you, the fact that you were born there, in the Panier, among the harbor dogs! And now you talk to me about Arabs!

And when she replies, "My blood's Italian. Italians aren't Arabs," Fabio explodes. "The South isn't Italy. It's the land of the wops. You know what the people in Piedmont call us? The

Mau Mau. That includes niggers, Gypsies, and all the wops south of Rome!"

For all the attraction that crime fiction has for those of us who still read for plot, it's curious that when we find a writer whose voice we respond to, a hero we care about, the action becomes almost secondary. Izzo is a sharp, complex plotter, but he can't resist indulging in descriptions of the pleasures the city offers. Food and music are integral. The sections on the proper way to desalt cod and the right wine to accompany a mid-morning snack of anchovy puree; the recipe for lasagna sauce to dress a fennel-stuffed bass: these are not digressions, not the cutesy gourmand asides that cozy up other mysteries. These passages are the living essence of the book, Proustian cues that summon Fabio's past, conjurations of the flavors, literal as well as figurative, that still haunt him. Each description of food or cooking is lovingly, tantalizingly drawn out, meant to convey a particular mixture of brininess and just-caught freshness, as well as the sense of pleasure that, like a good wine, comes with a long finish. "We launched on a major survey of foreign cuisines. Considering the number of restaurants between Aix and Marseilles, it was likely to take us many months . . . Top of our list was the Mille et une nuits . . . You sat on pouffes and ate from a big brass platter, listening to raï. Moroccan cuisine. The most refined in North Africa. They served the best pigeon *pastilla* I've ever tasted." Fabio, who narrates the books, even describes sex in terms of spices. For Izzo, those descriptions are a lover's testimony, whether the object of his ardor is Marseilles or one of the women by whom Fabio tries, doggedly but often futilely, to do justice.

If Izzo uses food to stand for the city's sensuality, he uses music to bring to life its ethnic jumble. The sounds wafting—or blaring—out of bars and clubs and radios and stereos come across less like a battle in which every voice is fighting to be heard than a din in which every voice finds the freedom to speak up. The glut of music may be the only real democracy in the city. The Arab and Algerian youths listen to Marseilles rappers IAM and the fabulous MC Solaar. "Marseilles was a place where people liked to talk a lot," says Fabio. "Rap was just talk, and lots of it. Our Jamaican cousins had brothers here. The rappers talked the way people talked in bars. About Paris, the centralized state, the decaying suburbs, the night buses. Their lives, their problems. The world, seen from Marseilles."

Rap isn't Fabio's music, but nearly everything else is. Among his touchstones are Miles Davis's *Sketches of Spain*, Dylan's *Nashville Skyline*, Sonny Rollins's *The Bridge* and Mongo Santamaría. Gypsy songs play in bars. Salsa provides the soundtrack for a night Fabio spends dancing with Marie-Lou, the prostitute who's his sometime lover. And the defeatist romantic melancholy that increasingly takes over the trilogy as it works toward its awful, devastating ending—a mood that can be traced right back to the 1937 film *Pépé le Moko*—is represented by the *chansons* of the anarchist singer-composer Léo Ferré (and occasionally by his contemporaries Georges Brassens and Jacques Brel). In *Chourmo*, Fabio finds an Algerian veteran beaten in his home, the old man's war medal, the symbol of belief that he would be accepted by the country he fought for, shoved into his mouth. The two of them find an unexpected connection in their shared love of Lili Boniche, the Algerian-Jewish singer whose music, with its African, Arab, Spanish and *chanson* influences, is its own melting pot. When the elderly gentleman hears the name, Fabio observes, "The old man smiled. For a moment he was lost in thought, lost, I was sure, in a place where life was good." And the music is verbal, too:

> As a child of the East, she considered that the French language was becoming a place where the migrant could draw together strands from all the lands through which he had passed and finally feel at

> home. The language of Rimbaud, Valéry and René Char would crossbreed, she asserted. It was the dream of a generation of North African immigrants. You already heard a strange kind of French spoken in Marseilles, a mixture of Provencal, Italian, Spanish and Arabic, with bits of slang thrown in. Speaking it, the kids understood each other perfectly well. At least on the streets.

One of the pities of Izzo's early death is that it deprived us of continuing to read him on the question of Arabs in Europe. His conclusions refuse the unexamined assumptions of both right and left and fail to satisfy either extreme, making his voice all the more valuable—and necessary.

As the exchange between Fabio and Gélou suggests, Izzo is alive to—and disgusted by—the prejudice that exists toward Arabs. His realization that, for many young immigrants, crime is not just a more profitable life but possibly the only work open to them puts his work in line with classic muckraking liberal melodrama. As a cop, Fabio is hounded by the fact that by the time he's aware of kids in trouble, it may be too late for them. They, and their parents, are caught between being immigrants in a land where you are despised and where no real opportunity awaits and a homeland that leaves you feeling just as much of an outcast. An Algerian man returns home in *Total Chaos* only to find that "Algeria wasn't his story anymore. It was a story that didn't interest him. The empty, neglected shops. The land, parceled out to former mujaheddin and left uncultivated. The deserted villages, turned in on their own misery."

There's an echo of this in *Chourmo*, of finding the foreign in the place that is supposed to feel like home. The young Arab girl whom Gélou rejected as a suitable girlfriend for her missing son has an older brother who has adopted Islamist militancy. He forces his mother to serve him with her eyes lowered and throws his sister out of the house because she's dating a non-Arab boy.

Had Izzo lived, he'd have had to navigate the line between the right wing's emboldened prejudice toward Arabs in the wake of 9/11 and the left's predilection for classifying people who stand up to the misogyny and homophobia of Islamism as tools of the right. The depth of feeling in the trilogy, the hatred of bullying in all its forms and most of all the tenderness with which Izzo writes of women suggest he'd have been more than up to the task. Someone as in love with Marseilles's multiplicity of culture as Izzo was could never fall for separatist rhetoric, no matter what progressive clothes it disguises itself in. The unattainable dream that haunts the Marseilles Trilogy is the pursuit of pluralism.

The Marseilles Trilogy may be the most lyrical hard-boiled writing yet. And if Izzo has earned a place in the ranks of the finest hard-boiled writers, it's worth noting that he's done it while largely avoiding the shining angel-*femme fatale* polarities of the genre. Even the women who turn out to be duplicitous are extended compassion, a willingness to comprehend the logic of their actions. Women found to be liars are, in detective fiction, usually treated as the most treacherous of creatures. By contrast, here is how Izzo writes of one woman who has just confessed her lies: "The most important thing, though, was that, free now of lies, [her eyes] were no longer indifferent. They'd become human. Full of pain, but also full of hope." The rest are written of so tenderly that their departure, sometimes just the threat of their departure, leaves wounds in stories that are already bleeding from the departure of others.

As the trilogy moves into the final book, the pleasures the book offers—food, music, sex, camaraderie, the pull of the sea—are increasingly overtaken by the dark undertow that has been waiting all along. *Solea* takes its name from the final track of Miles Davis's *Sketches of Spain*, one of the series of great albums Davis made in collaboration with arranger Gil Evans. Davis's trumpet, playing over Evans's steady, relentless orchestral pulse, the sound of a growing storm that will not break, is an insistently, even defiantly lonely sound. Sometimes it cries out in a single sustained note, sometimes it dies down in a muted passage that could be the muttering of a heartbroken man. It's anguished and discordant, soaring and battered, not so much accompanied by the music underneath as fighting it. Davis sounds as if he wants to join that music, and as if he knows he can't. As the piece rolls toward the end of its twelve-plus minutes, the drums become more prominent, and they could be a march into battle or honors played as a coffin is lowered into the ground. In his liner notes to the album, Nat Hentoff characterized it as possessing "the 'deep song' of flamenco and the cry of the blues." Whatever it is, it's the music of the Marseilles Trilogy, as vast and alluring and annihilating as Fabio's beloved Mediterranean, where the story comes to its close. But if novels need a written, instead of a musical, coda, the last lines of Godard's *Pierrot le fou*, spoken by characters who are already ghosts, will do:

She's found again
What? Eternity
It's the sea . . . run away
With the sun

The Blue and the Black

By Jean-Claude Izzo

Translated from the French
by Howard Curtis

In the beginning is the Book. And that moment in which Cain kills his brother Abel. In the blood of this fratricide, the Mediterranean gives us the first *noir* novel.

There may well have been other murders before this, but this one is written down, and establishes forever the singular problem of mankind: that crime is the driving force which, over the centuries, will govern relationships between people. Whoever they are. Masters or servants. Princes or emperors. Free men or slaves. In the beginning, indeed, all the motives for murder already existed. Envy, jealousy. Desire, fear. Money. Power. Hatred. Hatred of others. Hatred of the world.

That is the basis of all the Greek tragedies. In case we had forgotten, the chutzpah of Patrick Raynal, editor of Gallimard's *Série Noire*, was there to remind us. When he published Sophocles' *Oedipus Rex* in his famous series, some in the narrow circles of the publishing world thought he was joking. But he wasn't. Far from it.

It was an academic, Didier Malmaison, who adapted the Greek text into a *Série Noire* novel. This magnificent book, which opens with a classic *noir* scene—a stranger arrives in town, everyone watches him, closing their doors and windows as he passes, he crosses the street—can be read in one sitting. Like a real crime novel. "Well, if you look at it that way . . ." many teachers were forced to admit. Indeed, if you look at it that way, the line of descent from Greek tragedy to the *noir* novel becomes obvious. In *Oedipus* we witness a search for the truth of a man's life. In the *noir* novel, beginning with the Americans, the same process is developed, in parallel with an investigation into the social conditions of contemporary man, the modern form of fate. This is very clear in the works of David Goodis and Jim Thompson, who both deal with the tragedy of modern societies.

In a 1995 interview appearing in the review *Les Temps Modernes*, Patrick Raynal explained this lineage:

> If we can broadly define *noir* writing, *noir* inspiration, as a way of looking at the world, at the dark, opaque, criminal side of the world, shot through with the intense feeling of fatality we carry within us due to the fact that the only thing we know for certain is that we are going to die, then *Oedipus* can indeed be said to be the first *noir* novel.

James M. Cain, in *The Postman Always Rings Twice*, is another exponent of modern tragedy. I have not plucked Cain's name from the air. We now know that his work was a major influence on Albert Camus' *The Outsider*. The similarities are striking. A man, in no way predisposed to become a criminal, kills another man and finds himself in prison. Beneath the "stars in the night sky," he discovers the "benign indifference of the world," and his last wish, in order for the drama to be finally consummated, is "that there should be a crowd of spectators at [his] execution and that they should greet [him] with cries of hatred."

For me, *The Outsider* is the beginning of the modern Mediterranean crime novel. More so, in my opinion, than the novels of Manuel Vázquez Montalbán, who owes more, in both form and content, to Chandler and Hammett than to Cain. Today, there are many authors continuing this line of descent from Greek tragedy. The Spaniards Andreu Martín and

Francisco Gonzales Ledesma, the Italians Peppe Ferrandino, Nino Filasto, Santo Piazzese, Nicoletta Vallorani and Carlo Lucarelli, the Algerians Yasmina Khadra and Abdelkader Djemaï, and the Frenchmen René Frégni, Pascal Dessaint, Marcus Malte. All of them combine the viewpoint of Camus with that of Montalbán. The inspiration comes from this observation by Camus, in *Helen's Exile*:

Such moments make one realize that if the Greeks knew despair, they experienced it always though beauty and its oppressive quality. In this golden sadness, tragedy reaches its highest point. The despair of our world, on the other hand, has fed on ugliness and crisis. For which reason, Europe would be ignoble, if ever suffering could be.[1]

The Mediterranean crime novel is the fatalistic acceptance of this drama that has hung over us ever since man killed his brother on one of the shores of this sea.

Individual tragedy is echoed in the collective tragedy of the Balkans and Algeria, where the same dark blood flows. Faced with these conflicts which have punctuated the history of the Mediterranean, artists have tirelessly responded with their passion for the sea that unites. Paraphrasing Camus, I would call it a recognition of our ignorance, a rejection of fanaticism and of the limits of the world and of man, the beloved face, and beauty: that is the theatre in which we play out the same drama as the Greeks. And along with the other authors of these two shores, I affirm here, in the Mediterranean, in the name of a blue Mediterranean against a black Mediterranean, that the meaning of the history of tomorrow is "not what we think." Far from it.

[1] Albert Camus, *L'exil d'Hélène*, 1948

Monk Kept Going, Solo

By Valla Vakili

November 29, 2005: the day I finished the first volume of Jean-Claude Izzo's Marseilles trilogy, *Total Chaos*. For 248 pages I had traveled with Fabio Montale, the series protagonist, through his world. It was a world I didn't want to leave, but my French is non-existent and the second volume of the Trilogy, *Chourmo*, wasn't available in English translation yet. I found another way of continuing the story, though—one that eventually led to the creation of my company, Small Demons.

But that came later, and Montale's world came first.

When I first came across Izzo, I was looking specifically for crime fiction set outside my home town of Los Angeles, and ideally outside the States. I picked up *Total Chaos*, Leonardo Padura's *Havana Red*, and *Holy Smoke* by Tonino Benaquista. France, Cuba, France, and Italy, in that order. I've always been a sucker for great covers, and something about the cover of *Total Chaos* said, "read me first." So I did.

I dove into the world of Fabio Montale, a Marseilles cop who operates in that familiar noir territory of being so on the periphery of the police force that he can barely be said to be a part of it. I'd come across this character in other books, in other settings, by other writers.

There was something about Montale, though, that separated him from others who have played this role, and with whom I'd previously traveled through pages, cases, and stories. The difference was in the details of his world, and how easily I found myself connecting to him through these details. His fractured, dramatic relationships with women. His taste for single malt Scotch, for jazz and the blues. These I shared with him. But his love for Marseilles, for its food, its music, its streets and its sea—these were all new to me.

By the last passage of the first chapter, I knew that I had found in Montale a character I would follow anywhere:

> The message machine was flashing. It was late. Everything could wait. I'd just had a shower. I poured myself a Lagavulin, put on a Thelonius Monk album, and went to bed with Conrad's *Between the Tides*. My eyes closed. Monk kept going, solo.

Which is just what I did.

Prior to Montale, I had been a Laphroaig drinker. Nothing could make me switch my taste in Scotch. By the end of *Total Chaos*, I had drank as much Lagavulin as Montale, if not more. (I even returned to Oban, which had always given me an instant headache, only to find that I could drink it smoothly now. Just like Montale.) Along the way I had also listened to all the jazz and blues music cited in the book, and looked up everything I could about the local bands and writers he mentions throughout the story. On November 29, 2005 (I always mark the date I finish a book on the last page), when I had read the last word on the last page of *Total Chaos*, I was nowhere near done with Montale's story. His world had become part of my world. But I wanted more.

Chuormo wasn't available in English yet, so I did the only natural thing left for me to do. I went to Marseilles, where I spent a week with the food, the streets, the music, all the sights and sounds of Montale's world.

I returned from that trip convinced that great books are meant not only to be read and to exist in our minds, but also to be experienced. Many of the most compelling experiences available to us—to anyone craving something new and interesting—are locked within the life stories of great characters. At the time I was working for Yahoo! with the Entertainment group in Los Angeles. I ran around to everyone I knew, thumbing through my edition of *Total Chaos*, pointing to the Scotch, the jazz, the blues, the streets of Marseilles, trying to sell the same line: "These experiences are incredible. Too incredible to be locked in the book. We need to gather them all up and put them in one place, where any reader can enter the world of a character, of a story, and get lost in all its details."

It took four years, and another approach, until I found the way from Izzo to my company, Small Demons. Together with a designer friend I sketched out a website that would contain all the details inside a book on one page. We used *Total Chaos* as the example for this, and focused on the food, the books, the music, the Scotch. I took that design to the person who would later become my co-founder, and that was all it took.

Today, a couple years after that first site design, Small Demons features all the interesting people, places and things from each of ten thousand books captured in one place, with many more to come. The details of a story live on, beyond the printed page, for anyone who just can't get enough of a great character, and his or her world.

It's only natural, of course, that our origin can be traced back to the world of a single character type—the detective. As Chandler wrote of the detective in *The Simple Art of Murder*, "He must be the best man in his world and a good enough man for any world."

Over the course of the Marseilles trilogy—*Total Chaos, Chourmo,* and *Solea*—Fabio Montale is of course the best man in his world. This much Izzo knew. But he was also a good enough man to call forth all the details of every man in every world, in every work of fiction, as we seek to do at Small Demons.

And every time I drink Lagavulin, I think of him.

Valla Vakili
Co-Founder and CEO
Small Demons

Andrea Camilleri on Jean-Claude Izzo

From an interview with Andrea Camilleri
by Brigida Corrado

I was in a bookstore. It was the title that got my attention: *Total Chaos*. I read the jacket copy, which intrigued me, and bought the book. When I finished it I was flabbergasted because I felt like I had made a real discovery. I went back to the bookstore and picked up *Chourmo*, the second book in the "Marseilles trilogy." I couldn't find *Solea* but I promised myself I would read all of this author's books. His ability to describe Marseilles and to make his readers feel the multiracial reality of that city so directly and authentically was fascinating . . . It was better that reading ten sociological essays. And, though he never lost sight of this larger purpose, the author tipped his hat in the direction of two things that really impressed me: his roots as a Mediterranean man, a man of the south; and, the poems of Saint-John Perse. He slips in references to this very powerful though not well known poet with extreme naturalness and refinement.

I tell you, it was like falling in love, something that happens to me rarely.

A year later I went to the *salon du livre* in Paris and while I was at my publisher's booth (prisoner or sideshow act, as you will) a man comes up to me and says, "Hello, I'm Jean-Claude Izzo." He had no inkling of my love affair. I embraced him and said: "Holy crap, this is the greatest meeting of my life." We hit it off instantly, and in the afternoon, we were joined by Manuel Vázquez Montalbán. It was a wonderful afternoon. I so admired Izzo's discretion and his generally delicate approach to the world . . . I didn't know him well, but the impression he left me with was one of purity, simplicity, goodness. We spent three days together, in each other's company the whole time. He presented me with a French edition of his trilogy, the Gallimard box set, and we promised we'd see each other again soon . . .

Some time after that, he contacted me to ask me if I'd be willing to present his books in Italy. Obviously, I said yes without a thought. He even told me when, more or less, it would be. Then I lost contact with him. As we drew nearer the date of the presentation I contacted his publisher because I hadn't heard any more from Jean-Claude. They told me he was very sick. It was a terribly hard knock for me—when I'd met him in Paris he was fine.

Not long after that, I was told about his death.

At a certain age it's difficult to make new friends and I think Izzo and I could have been great friends. He would have enriched my life. I still regret that things didn't turn out that way. His death was a real loss for me.

I loved him because he was a writer who took a stand—I cannot love someone who doesn't take sides. And, whereas there are no similarities between Pepe Carvalho and Montalbano (not only because of the ways they cook and eat), there is a strong and meaningful connection between Montalbano and Fabio Montale. Neither can stand racism nor power.

My favorite book? *The Lost Sailors*. The writing is divine. And I liked a book of occasional writings entitled *Garlic, Mint & Sweet Basil* very much. It's a real delight.

"Mediterranean noir" is an approach. Only fools still think of it as genre fiction. The Mediterranean noir novel is engaged, it indicts and demands accountability. It is not a minor work of genre fiction. If readers paid more attention to the messages brought to them by noir novels our society would be a better place.

The Yellow and the Black

By Tobias Jones

In 1976, a 19-year-old student radical and member of *Lotta Continua* named Massimo Carlotto was accused of a murder he didn't commit. A pawn in the struggle between *Lotta Continua* and the police, he was arrested, tried and just before sentence was pronounced, his lawyer advised him to run. He escaped to Paris and ended up in Mexico, where, in 1985, he was betrayed by a Mexican lawyer and extradited to Italy. Retried, he was found guilty and imprisoned until, in 1993, he was pardoned by the President.

Carlotto is now almost 50, a good-looking, beefy man, normally photographed with a cigar poking out from greying stubble. Last year a film about his life called *Il Fuggiasco* (*The Fugitive*) came out in Italy. Since his release, Carlotto has reinvented himself as a writer of hugely popular thrillers. More than merely hard-boiled, his novels are sexy, seedy, cynical, and nihilistic, but with moments of idealism. Thanks in part to Carlotto, noir has become the boom genre of Italian publishing. Einaudi have introduced two new imprints, *Stile libero* and *Stile libero Noir*. The Sicilian publisher Sellerio is permanently at the top of the bestseller lists thanks to the octogenarian Andrea Camilleri, whose books have also been stylishly adapted for television. Carlo Lucarelli—co-editor of *Stile libero Noir* and another bestselling writer of thrillers—fronts a TV programme about real murder cases.

The Italian public seem permanently hungry for "*gialli.*" In bookshops you find shelf on shelf of Follett and Forsyth translations, as well as Italian thrillers. And when it comes to real-life *gialli*, practically every news programme announces "a gripping new thriller unravelling" somewhere. *Sub judice* is ignored as bloodstains, bullet holes, and murder weapons are shown, and reporters chase mourning mothers down the street, microphone in hand. As Hitchcock once said, "television has brought murder back into the home—where it belongs."

The greatest asset of the Italian thriller is that the reader doesn't need to suspend disbelief. So many astonishing and intricate crimes seem to take place in the country that the fictional ones appear perfectly probable. In some thrillers, fictional mysteries are blended in with real ones. Carlotto, in his novels, hovers between reality and invention. In the postscript to *The Colombian Mule*[1], he describes the man on whom one of the characters is based and outlines the techniques he and his fellow prisoners used to protect themselves from sexual predators ("two of us would wash while the third stood guard, a bathrobe rolled round his left arm and the handle of a frying pan, filed to razor sharpness, clasped in his right hand"). In an author's note at the end of *The Shape of Water*[2], Camilleri says that his book is fiction, even though "in recent years reality has seemed bent on surpassing the imagination, if not entirely abolishing it."

The emphasis on realism means that many Italian thrillers avoid neat resolutions. Miss Marple moments, when the entire cast is assembled and the detective delivers a tidy summary, are rare. In Italian whodunnits one may discover who did it, but—a reflection of Italian reality—the criminal is rarely collared; the writer gives you the satisfaction of solving the crime, but withholds the pleasure of letting you see justice done. Carlotto

[1] *The Colombian Mule* by Massimo Carlotto trans. Christopher Woodall · Orion.

[2] *The Shape of Water* by Andrea Camilleri trans. Stephen Sartarelli · Picador.

echoes the pessimism of many Italians: "The law is nothing but a cover for the petty vendettas and back-stabbing of a collection of state spooks." Italy, he writes, "has lost any sense of where truth lies."

"No one cared about knowing the truth," says the narrator of Marcello Fois's *The Advocate.*[3] "It was easier that way, it didn't tread on the toes of important people."

The criminal cases in many of these *gialli* have been settled before the action begins. The narrative isn't about closing, but about reopening a case, reinterpreting it. Camilleri's world-weary Sicilian detective, Montalbano, invariably has to battle against his superiors' desire for a quick "archiving" of a case; in *The Colombian Mule* the detective is hired not to put someone in prison, but to get him out. In *The Advocate*, a peasant has been found guilty in absentia and only a dogged lawyer can get him off. Most Anglo-Saxon detective fiction is concerned with justice: the Italian version tends, more interestingly, to focus on injustice. In all these thrillers evidence is deliberately lost, witnesses disappear, there is political interference, and the Mafia code of silence—*omertà*—is observed. "In a country full of unanswered questions," Lucarelli said in an interview with *La Repubblica* recently, thrillers "have an ever more passionate and numerous public."

In all this, Carlotto and his colleagues are the inheritors of a noble tradition. Loriano Macchiavelli, Leonardo Sciascia, and Fruttero and Lucentini have all managed in the past to combine absorbing plots with meditations on the state of the nation and its susceptibility to illusion. Sciascia in particular understood what his fellow Sicilian Pirandello called the "marvellous torment" of ambiguity. Moral labels like "honourable" and "gentleman" are attached all too loosely in Sicily, and Sciascia

[3] *The Advocate: A Sardinian Mystery* by Marcello Fois trans. Patrick Creagh · Vintage.

toyed with that looseness in his fiction and exported it to the mainland. By now, the suspicion of clear-cut moral distinctions is so deep that whenever an *onorevole*—an MP—is described in fiction you can be sure he's doing something dishonourable. Once the genie of cynicism was out of the bottle, it became impossible to distinguish appearance from reality or suspicion from paranoia. "I find you all exhausted from your search to find out who and what other people are," a character in Pirandello says. This uncertainty makes for sophisticated exercises in detection and carries the fiction far beyond the mere investigation of a crime. As Sciascia has it, Sicilians, like Jews, speak "by allusion, in parable or in metaphors. It was as if the same circuits, the same logical processes operated in both their minds. A computer of distrust, of suspicion, of pessimism."

Giallo isn't the right word for these novels: it makes them sound too cheap. The writers themselves prefer "noir" and there is nothing unreasonable in that. The most self-conscious stylist among them is Lucarelli. In *Almost Blue*[4], a serial killer is on the loose in Bologna, but the police psychologists are bewildered: the killer appears to change identity with each murder. Only the voice remains the same. The hero, Simone, is a blind recluse, who listens closely to sounds and voices.

The sound of a record dropping onto a turntable is like a short sigh, with a touch of dust mixed in. The sound of the automated arm rising up from its rest is like a repressed hiccup or a tongue clucking dryly—a plastic tongue. The needle, as it glides across the grooves, sibilates softly and crackles once or twice. Then comes the piano, a dripping tap. Then, the bass, buzzing like an enormous fly at a window.

Mood is modulated by speech patterns, by breathing, sighs and glottal stops. Simone inhabits a synaesthetic world:

[4] *Almost Blue* by Carlo Lucarelli trans. Oonagh Stransky · Harvill.

> Colour comes from the way a person breathes through their words. From the pressure of their breath. If the pressure is low, they're sad, anxious or needy. If the pressure is high, they're sincere, ironic or good-natured. If the pressure is even, they're either indifferent or conclusive. If the pressure increases all of a sudden, they're threatening, vulgar or violent. If the pressure fluctuates and gets rounded out on the corners, then they're being affectionate, malicious or sensual.

One night Simone hears something sinister and contacts Detective Inspector Grazia Negro, and the two attempt to trace a single voice in the "two thousand square kilometres" of the Bolognese metropolis.

"All I ever wanted was to be a blues singer," says Carlotto's private eye, the Alligator. His is a Chandleresque world in which gruff good guys return home at sunrise, probably still wearing suits and trilbies. They smoke and drink too much; their relationships are falling apart. The Alligator is a nightclub owner whose nickname comes from his favourite drink: "seven parts Calvados to three of Drambuie . . . a lot of ice and a slice of green apple to chew on once I've emptied the glass. It's called an Alligator and was invented by a barman in Cagliari, to add a little joy to my life." The society represented is pretty sordid. Political idealism is a thing of the past. "The left has been marginalised for good," Carlotto writes wistfully. "It's not our world any longer. For a brief moment, we held it in the palm of our hand. Then they snatched it away again."

The case revolves around a Colombian cocaine smuggler stopped at Venice airport. The police let him go and track him in order to capture his Italian contact, and duly arrest an art smuggler, Nazzareno Corradi, who has rushed to the drug smuggler's hotel after an anonymous phone call has told him that his Colombian girlfriend is there and seriously ill. The defence lawyer calls the Alligator in to help establish Corradi's innocence. His actions are hampered by the moral code of the underworld: no grassing and all that. In order to find out who the real contact was he needs to uncover the channels used by the smugglers and so tries to buy and offload his own stash of coke. The trail leads not to the criminal underworld but to the police. All the good/bad roles are reversed. Religious statues from South America are containers for coke. Prison guards are cooperative, given the right amount of alcohol and a few compliant women. The moral is that it's better to be an honest crook than a bent copper. Carlotto is grinding his axe, but it doesn't really matter. He is too much of a realist to allow the release of Corradi, a criminal who is, on this occasion, innocent. The case is solved but the real crooks remain at large.

Camilleri's Inspector Salvo Montalbano is a good cop, and his novels are more *giallo* than noir. They come with glossaries: every page is peppered with Sicilian dialect that the average Italian struggles to understand. There's a lightness of touch in his descriptions, an almost playful tone, even though, as with Sciascia, the crimes often involve the political class. In several recent interviews, Camilleri has attacked Berlusconi and his Sicilian cadres, and that hostility seeps into his fiction. "In Sicily," he writes, echoing Lampedusa, "and in the province of Montelusa in particular, *mutatis mutandis*—or *zara zabara*, to say it in Sicilian—things never budged, even when there was a storm on the horizon."[5] He quoted, with obvious facility, the prince of Salina's famous statement about changing everything in order to change nothing.

Camilleri writes shrewdly about Italian society, from its obsession with food—"as they ate, they spoke of eating, as

[5] *The Terra-Cotta Dog* by Andrea Camilleri trans. Stephen Sartarelli · Penguin.

always happens in Italy"—to the vertiginous cynicism of the Communist broadcaster who nurtures a scandal not by exposing it but by remaining ostentatiously silent. "Let me explain, my innocent friend. The quickest way to make people forget a scandal is to talk about it as much as possible, on television, in the papers and so on. Over and over you flog the same dead horse, and pretty soon people start getting fed up . . . if, on the other hand, you hush everything up, the silence itself starts to talk, rumours begin to multiply out of control until you can't stop them any more."

Like Camilleri, Fois is interested in the character of the place he comes from—in his case, Sardinia—and the way in which it is misunderstood by outsiders. Set in the aftermath of the Risorgimento, *The Advocate* takes place as the island is being colonised, having modernity imposed on it by people from the mainland. A peasant is accused of stealing sheep and murdering the farmer; everyone is already convinced of his guilt. Only a poor lawyer, Bustianu, is prepared to identify the real murderers. The book has the narrative minimalism of a biblical parable, yet this Sardinia is a barren, godless land; the landscape is the "sole divinity":

> And behold me again, pierced to the heart by such a wealth of beauty, and stunned by it, all but overcome. The immensity of it is beyond words: immensity battering at frailty! A sublimity that catches you in the heart . . . I take a deep breath and feel that all that blue light, that green, and the rolling stubble-fields, make their secret way into my body and stream lines of poetry into my mind. Words like deep breaths and lips that tremble when my eyes light upon such colours. For this land is to me both my joy and my torment. It lures me to it yet thrusts me off. And I curse it, I curse even while I worship it. O cruel woman, embracing mother, insatiable love!

Everything appears yielding and yet forbidding, all eloquence is a form of reticence and silence. The task of the advocate is to persuade the peasants to share their knowledge with him. In Fois, the detective is usually the last to know; like the murdered man, he is a victim of the plot.

And that, presumably, is why these books have been so successful in Italy: they chime perfectly with the average reader's (often justified) paranoia. They re-create the conspiracy of silence but manage, in whispered hints, to talk over it.

"I'M NOT INTERESTED IN THE GOOD GUYS WINNING"

Massimo Carlotto interviewed by Brian Oliver[1]

In prison for a murder he didn't commit, Massimo Carlotto found the true-life material for his explicit crime novels that go to the corrupt heart of Italy.

You couldn't make it up. A schoolboy starts thinking about politics at a very young age, joins the local boy scouts and turns ultra-left. In Padova, northeast Italy, in the late 1960s, the boy scouts were a hotbed of radicalism.

By the age of thirteen, he is active in the *Lotta Continua*, a left-wing group, and becomes a reporter for its weekly newspaper. At 19, during Italy's "years of lead," when political tensions were at their highest, he witnesses a brutal murder. Carlotto is arrested for the crime. Three years later, after he has been acquitted, retried, and convicted—there is no double jeopardy in Italian law—he is sentenced to 18 years. He goes on the run to France, then Mexico City.

For six years, he is sheltered, fed, and educated by political activists before giving himself up back in Italy. His battle with the courts becomes one of the most famous cases in Italian law: eighty judges and magistrates are involved; he is tried and retried eleven times; the case drags on for eighteen years; his legal paperwork weighs ninety-six kilos. Eventually, after an international campaign, a Scotland Yard expert says the foren-

[1] This interview first appeared in *The Observer*, January 30, 2005. It appears in this publication with kind permission of *The Guardian Newspaper*.

sic procedures used in the case are twenty years out of date and the President of Italy pardons him.

As a free man, he turns to writing. After an autobiography, newspaper articles, essays, and plays, he turns to crime writing, inventing a character based on himself called the "Alligator," an unlicensed investigator who drinks too much calvados and drives a Škoda.

Two of his books are made into films, and a third, *The Dark Immensity of Death*, produced by Aurelio De Laurentiis, is on the way. He has a huge following in Italy and France and is about to test the British market. He now lives in Quartu Sant'Elena, just outside Cagliari, in Sardinia with his wife, Colomba, and two-year-old son Giovanni. "I'll make sure I send him to the scouts," he says, laughing.

You couldn't make it up. You wouldn't have to because that, in brief, is the life story of Massimo Carlotto.

We meet in a gastropub in east London. I'm expecting someone weighed down by his troubled past, but Carlotto proves an engaging conversationalist with a penchant for self-deprecation. Rugged, stubbly (he has lots of female fans), he is simply dressed in dark clothes. Now forty-eight, he has the impressive physique of an ex-rugby player (and he probably weighs a few kilos more than his legal history).

Judging by the detailed description of what Alligator and his friends eat between stakeouts—pappardelle with chicken livers and a suitable vintage, baccalà, an elaborate pumpkin risotto—one would assume that Carlotto missed a decent meal while in prison.

"Not at all," he says, lighting up the first of a series of black cigars. "I was in with the right people, *mafiosi* who, because of their connections, were able to buy privileges. They could get decent produce, so they spent a great deal of time planning a menu and cooking. To put it succinctly, you could say I ate a lot of very lavish Sicilian and Calabrian meals."

Carlotto made good use of his time inside. He was a negotiator between rival factions, made valuable friends from the world of organised crime as a "scribe," writing letters and documents for fellow prisoners. And now he uses those contacts from the criminal world to add more than a touch of reality to some of the most hardcore material on the crime shelves. A leading member of the "Mediterranean Noir" group who lament the lack of investigative journalism in Italy and, to a lesser extent, France and Spain, Carlotto says his novels are all based on real criminals, real killings, real life. His graphic descriptions of gruesome deaths—from a straightforward shooting and throat-slitting to an arranged car crash, an impaling on a lance and murder by fist-fucking—offer an insight into the company Carlotto keeps, or kept, the friends he made "inside."

"I have never once made up a killing," he says. "Every single death in everything I have written relates to a real killing, one for which I have read the autopsy report. I have seen the documents, I have carried out one-to-one interviews with murderers. This is my way of recording what is happening in present-day Italy.

"The Noir writers talk about the social and political situation right now; they react very quickly to changes in the criminal world. In Italy, Mediterranean Noir is called the literature of reality. I even have journalists calling me when they are writing about crime, to ask me what is going on. The world of journalism has changed. There is no investigation now. Italy has lost any real sense of truth, because nobody believes the official 'truths.'

"It is very rare now for crime writers [in Italy] to invent stories. Most of them are real. Only the names are changed. That's why these books are so popular."

Carlotto reckons there are about a dozen writers in the Mediterranean Noir movement. Two of them have died in the past four years, but their work is published in English—Jean-Claude Izzo, a French-Italian whom Carlotto rates best of all, and the Catalan Manuel Vázquez Montalbán. If Carlotto sells well in translation, then more Noir writers will be translated. The most popular is Andrea Camilleri, the Sicilian whose books sell 200,000-300,000 in Italy; Carlotto's sales figures are not far behind.

Imprisoned crime writers are not rare in Latin America, where Carlotto has family and many friends. The biggest name in English-language crime writing who spent years behind bars is Edward Bunker, the American who was in prison for around thirty years in various institutions for a series of crimes he did commit. Carlotto has never met Bunker but has read all his works and is a fan.

Whether "reality crime" from the Mediterranean will prove popular in the English-speaking world should become clear this year, with a second Carlotto book about to be published. Since Henning Mankell won the Gold Dagger, the top crime award in British publishing, in 2001, there has been a Euro-boom. Maxim Jakubowski, author, critic, and owner of Murder One, the London specialist bookstore, reckons sales of translated works have gone up five-fold in recent years. The cultural differences—not least language—the sense of place, the strengths and weaknesses of a variety of investigating agencies, and the depth of character in many works can make Euro-crime far more rewarding than, for example, mainstream American books.

The Colombian Mule[2], Carlotto's 2001 novel about drug smuggling and police vengeance, was published in the UK last year. The second, *The Master of Knots*[3], is set against a backdrop of police brutality at the anti-capitalist demonstrations at

[2] *The Colombian Mule* by Massimo Carlotto trans. Christopher Woodall · Orion.

[3] *THe Master of Knots* by Massimo Carlotto trans. Christopher Woodall · Orion.

the G8 summit in Genoa in 2001 and explores the darkest depths of S&M, disappearing parents, snuff movies and prostitution. It is based on a real case, the details of which were sent to Carlotto by a reader's email that started: "Dear Alligator."

Carlotto accepts that his own leading characters are far from pleasant. Is it really so grim underneath the surface of life in modern Italy? "Yes, but you have to bear in mind that things have changed.

Alongside the changes in the global economy there has been a revolution in the criminal world, too." According to a United Nations report five years ago, he says, the worldwide annual income from organised crime is measured in thousands of billions of dollars, and the biggest problem for criminals is laundering the money.

"The most popular area for recycling is the Mediterranean, because of the well-developed relationship between the various mafias and banking, industry and politics. In the richest part of Italy, the northeast, there is very close interweaving between the legal economy and the black economy. The very top levels of the underworld have realised that they have to infiltrate the productive manufacturing process. They have to work with others, and the balance between different mafia organisations has changed, producing different strata, different cultural layers.

"While the Sicilian Mafia has retracted to the south, the Nigerians have become heavily involved in drugs, the Romanians run prostitution, the Chinese and Croatians have their sweatshops and at a lower level you have the Albanians. There is a completely new situation regarding organised crime."

There are new rules, too. The old-style Mafia "code of honour"—never grass, never steal a friend's girl, and so on—no longer applies, he says. And he should know, since his best source of information is an old-style Mafia man. Other sources include lawyers, readers, the majority of whom, he says, are women, and, occasionally, police officers.

There are three main characters in the Alligator series. The "brains" is a computers and information geek who drinks too much, cooks sumptuous meals, rarely goes out and holds extreme left-wing views. The muscle is provided by Rossini, based on Carlotto's real-life top criminal source, who never shirks from a cold-blooded execution. Then there's the Alligator himself: nightclub owner, blues and jazz fan, always in search of "the truth."

"I develop the plots out of actual legal cases, legal errors," says Carlotto, sipping an espresso. "The Alligator is a kind of loser who uses his skills in the service of other losers."

What about the casual way in which the perceived "good guys" will execute opponents? "I'm not interested in the good guys winning and the bad guys losing," he says. "There's innocence and innocence . . . I'm interested in reality, and this is real."

Even down to the choice of car. Not many hard-nuts would be seen behind the wheel of a Škoda, but the Alligator drives one—and Carlotto did, too, "but my wife won't let me now, so it's a Citroën"—because the Škoda is the car least stopped by police on Italy's roads.

His wife is an accountant in the local tax office and he is just about to open a bookshop in Quartu, because there isn't one and will be running writing courses from the shop. His only weakness seems to be a passion for calvados. "Everyone knows about whisky, grappa, no one knows about calvados." He drinks a cocktail named the Alligator, after his character, invented by a barman in Cagliari—three parts Drambuie, seven parts calvados, served with lots of crushed ice and a slice of green apple "to eat and console yourself when the glass is empty." "Nobody can drink more than four, and nobody ever has." The fame of this cocktail has spread and you can now get an Alligator at bars in Rome, Milan and Naples.

The conversation turns serious. Did Carlotto ever give up hope during those lost years, most of them spent in maximum security, thinking: "I'll be an old man before I'm out. I'm in here for life"?

"Twenty-four hours a day," he says.

Whom does he hold responsible for the loss of so much life: a corrupt policeman, a political opponent, a judge? "*Il sistema*," he says. The legal system that he, and his supporters, helped to change. It still has its faults. In the 1980s, Cesare Battisti, another Italian writer, was sentenced to life imprisonment for terrorism, in absentia, under special laws. He has always pleaded innocence but is now himself a fugitive because the French government has agreed to an extradition request from Italy. Carlotto is among those campaigning for Battisti's freedom.

Many of Carlotto's generation were wrongly imprisoned, he says, always because of their politics. Carlotto would have been cleared immediately had a proper forensic investigation taken place in 1976. He is still waiting. A hair from under the victim's fingernails, which would have given a DNA sample, mysteriously "disappeared" from a safe at the coroner's office. This is one case even the Alligator could not solve.

My Strange Policeman Friend

By Carlo Lucarelli

I was supposed to graduate from Bologna University with a thesis in contemporary history on the police during the fascist period. I don't remember well what studies had brought me there, but I was collecting material for a thesis entitled "The Vision of the Police in the Memories of Anti-Fascists" when I ran across a strange character who in a certain sense changed my life.

He was a policeman who had spent forty years in the Italian police, from 1941 to 1981, when he retired. He had started in the fascist political police, the OVRA, a secret organization the meaning of whose very acronym was never known with certainty. As an "ovrino," he told me, his job was to tail, to spy on, and to arrest anti-fascists who were plotting against the regime. Later, still as an ovrino, he was to tail, to spy on, and to arrest those fascists who disagreed with fascism's leader, Benito Mussolini. During the war, his job went back to tailing, spying on, and arresting anti-fascist saboteurs, but towards the end of the war, when part of liberated Italy was under the control of partisan formations fighting alongside the Allies, my strange policeman friend actually became part of the partisan police. As he was good, he told me, he had never done anything particularly brutal and the partisans needed professionals like him to ensure public order and safety. Naturally, his duties included arresting fascists who had stained themselves with criminal acts during the war. Several years later, when, following elections, a regular government was formed in Italy, our policeman became part of the Italian Republic's police; his job, to tail, to spy on, and to arrest some of those partisans who had been his colleagues and who were now considered dangerous subversives.

That encounter, and the studies I was undertaking at that moment, opened my eyes to a period that is fundamental in the history of Italy: strange, complicated and contradictory, as were the final years of the fascist regime in Italy.

Benito Mussolini and the fascists took power in October, 1922. For twenty years, the regime consolidated itself into a ferocious dictatorship that suspended political and civil liberties, dissolved parties and newspapers, persecuted opponents and put practically all of Italy in uniform, like what was happening in the meantime in Hitler's Germany. The outbreak of World War II saw Italy allied with Nazi Germany, but a series of military defeats, the hostility of a people exhausted by the war effort, and the landing of the Anglo-American forces in Sicily in 1943, brought about the fall of the fascist regime. Mussolini was arrested and, on September 8, the new government decided to break the alliance with Hitler and carry on the war alongside the Allies.

At this point, Italy splits in two as the German Army occupies that part of the country not yet liberated by the advance of the Anglo-American forces and puts Benito Mussolini in charge of a collaborationist government. This is one of the hardest and most ferocious moments in Italy's history. There is the war stalled on the North Italian front, where there is fierce fighting, for at least a year. There is dread of the *Brigate Nere*, the Black Brigades, and the formations of the new fascist government's political police who, together with the German SS, repress sabotage activities and resistance by partisan formations. There is, above all, enormous moral and political confusion that combines the desperation of those who know they are losing, the opportunism of those ready to change sides, the guilelessness of those who haven't understood anything, and even the desire for revenge in those who are about to arrive.

Only a couple of years, until April, 1945, when the war in Italy ends, but two ferocious, bloody, and above all confusing years, as I learned thanks to my studies and the accounts of my policeman friend. In Milan alone, for example, there were at least sixteen different police forces, from the regular police, the "Questura," to the Gestapo, each doing as they pleased and sometimes arresting one another.

But above all, I understood one thing from that encounter. For, after having heard that man recount forty years of his life in the Italian political police, during which with every change of government he found himself having to tail, to spy on, and to arrest those who had previously been his bosses, the question came spontaneously to me: "Excuse me, Maresciallo, but . . . who do you vote for?" And he, with equal spontaneity, responded: "What does that have to do with it? I'm a policeman." As if to say: I don't take political stands. I do. I am a technician, a professional, not a politician.

At that point, I thought that there are moments in the life of a country in which the technicians and the professionals are also asked to account for their political choices and non-choices. I thought about what my policeman friend would have done if things had gone differently. And to ask oneself what would have happened if is the spring that triggers the idea for a novel. So I started writing *Carte Blanche*. I invented Commissario De Luca, protagonist of *Carte Blanche*, *The Damned Season* and *Via delle Oche*, and lost myself in his adventures.

And I never did write my thesis.

On Writing Irish Crime

By Gene Kerrigan

For a long time, reading crime fiction was for me about mysteries and thrills, quirky private eyes, jaded cops and snappy dialogue. Diverting enough, up to a point—and that point was usually where the story turned sentimental. Richard Stark (aka Donald Westlake) changed that.

Stark was something new. His protagonist, Parker, was a professional criminal, a capable man with a limited view of life. The novels didn't offer empathy, they didn't allow for redemption. They just described, in blunt, stripped-down language, the behaviour of someone to whom crime was as natural as breathing. Parker lived a banal life, in resort hotels. Once or twice a year he committed a robbery, to replenish his accounts.

Parker hurt people when violence made things go more smoothly; he killed people when they became a problem. He didn't kill without reason—that was stupid, a killing made the cops work harder.

He didn't see himself as a bad man, or a good man. He was an amoral man who did what he needed to do to get ahead.

It wasn't much of a leap to see Parker's world view in the behaviour of all sorts of people—from Main Street to Wall Street to the back rooms where politicians make deals.

By and by I read all the Stark novels, most of them with garish packaging (some had imitation bullet holes punched in the front cover). Back then, in the seventies, such material was seen as paperback trash. Today the Parker novels are republished by the University of Chicago Press, and advertised in the *New York*

Review of Books. And the covers sometimes carry a quote from John Banville, claiming Stark is one of the "greatest writers of the twentieth Century." Banville has described Parker as "existential man at his furthest extremity, confronting a world that is even more wicked and treacherous than he is," and that's about right.

I found it hard, after Stark, to settle for formula fiction and cutesy dialogue. Later there was George V. Higgins and Elmore Leonard and Charles Willeford, George Pelecanos and Dennis Lehane. In the phrase used by Raymond Chandler about Dashiell Hammet—maybe this stuff was made up, but it was "made up out of real things." Entertaining, yes, but more than that.

My first attempt at a crime novel, in the eighties, was a pitiful effort. It was set in America. I'd been in the States often enough to get away with setting a story there, and in those days a crime novel set in Dublin wouldn't ring true. There was little organised crime in Ireland; most murders were assaults that got out of hand.

I got perhaps a third of the way into the story when I realised my novel amounted to little more than an embarrassing 30,000 words searching vainly for a purpose. I abandoned it.

The seven books I wrote or co-wrote over the next twenty years were non-fiction, usually involving themes I pursued in my journalism. Eventually I decided I knew enough about fiction to try again.

By then, 2005, Ireland had changed dramatically. German and UK and French banks were shovelling billions into Irish banks, which in turn shovelled some of the billions in the direction of property developers, who went on a building spree—houses, hotels, offices, trophy buildings galore. The rest of the borrowed money was loaned to the unfortunates who needed to buy houses in a market where prices were skyrocketing.

After decades of high unemployment and emigration, the country was awash with cash. Someone called the economy the "Celtic Tiger" and a lot of people began believing their own propaganda.

When the bubble burst, the German and UK and French banks faced losses of billions of Euros. But, to the astonishment of international observers, the Irish government decided it should pay the gambling debts of the foolish Irish banks. The private debt was shifted onto the citizens. And the state began cutting public services, to balance the books.

So, the era of imaginary wealth came to an abrupt halt, and the era of very real austerity arrived. It makes for an extraordinary story arc. Money washing through a society, then abruptly ebbing.

Whether it's Chicago in the twenties, London in the fifties or Moscow in the nineties, where there's a tide of money there will be people who think up new ways to spend it, new ways to steal it. In Ireland, in the boom years, the banking whiz-kids needed their cocaine. The kids on the fringes of society needed their heroin. The ghetto entrepreneurs went to work. Their mergers and acquisitions departments were busy, which meant that bodies were soon turning up in laneways, on canal banks and in the grass beside the quiet roads behind the airport.

There were now organised crime gangs in Dublin and in Limerick, conspiracies, assassinations, feuds. With these people, when you go out of business it's not because you lose market share, it's because someone turns up at your front door wearing a motorcycle helmet and carrying a sawed-off shotgun. I live in a quiet neighbourhood. A ten minute walk north of my home, a man was shot dead in a pub. A five minute walk to the east, a man was shot dead in a bookie shop. We now have bent cops, endless inquiries into complex banking deceit, a former minister for justice who went to jail for tax fraud—at least one politician who got away despite a questionable relationship to some gangsters.

Calamity for society. But these days, Irish crime fiction writers don't have to set their stories in far-off cities.

As a journalist, I had for a couple of decades observed Dublin's small-time hoods, the people who earn less from a life of crime than they'd make in a reasonably-paid job. My first published novel, *Little Criminals*, featured four of them, trying to step up from their small-time robberies, to get a cut of the wealth they saw all around them in Celtic Tiger Ireland.

Three more novels have followed, so far. Each tells a stand-alone story, but they cover the period 2005 to 2011 and in the background you can see what's happening to Ireland. *Little Criminals* is about greed, the conflict between old and new Ireland, the urge to grab a slice of the good life, whatever the cost to others. *The Midnight Choir* is about a self righteous policeman, unaware of his own corruption. *Dark Times in the City* is about a decent man swept up in the cruel world of gang warfare. *The Rage* is about a man rejecting his own responsibility when things go wrong, and seeking to put the blame elsewhere.

If you wanted to see the parallels, you could; a society that comes to believe that greed is good, proud of its victories and ignoring the corruption within; a society suddenly in trouble, shifting the responsibility to its weakest.

But the books weren't written as an analysis of a society's rise and fall—that's not how crime fiction works. It tends not to describe a society but to reflect it. The books are about the characters and their stories, against a background of a country that's aware of its shameful past and worried about its uncertain future.

(Anyone wanting a descriptive novel of Ireland's old/new conflicts, and the effects on society of economic collapse is referred to Donal Ryan's sad, wonderful, kaleidoscopic novel *The Spinning Heart*.)

With journalism, the story is told from the outside. You assemble the available information and find a structure through which to tell the tale. No matter how good a reporter you are, you can't get into the heads of the protagonists. With fiction, you tell the story from the inside. Either way, the aim is one that writers have always had: to say, this is who we are and these are the things we do.

In the Lost Realm of the Real

By Carl Bromley

Originally published in The Nation[1]

For Aurelio Zen, the urbane detective creation of the English writer Michael Dibdin, a few fateful weeks in Rome in 1978 changed everything. At the time Zen was on a career fast track. He had a top post in the kidnapping section of the Rome Questura (police headquarters) with the prospect of further promotion to *vice-questore* (deputy chief), perhaps even to *questore*. But then a combination of factors—his curiosity and sense of justice and a glimpse of the "secret center" of the Italian state—destroyed it all.

When the Red Brigades kidnap former Italian prime minister and Christian Democratic Party kingpin Aldo Moro, He is thrown into the investigation under the direction of Rome's Political Branch. Zen is incredulous to find that a department flush with government money "claimed to have no material on the terrorists beyond a few isolated descriptions and photographs." Zen and his colleague are reduced to conducting house-to-house searches, work that takes them to a part of Rome that's too close for the comfort of their superiors. His partner dies mysteriously, and when Zen narrows in on what his partner had discovered, he is intercepted by "the Politicals" for whom he is supposedly working. He is told, with classic bureaucratic terseness, that his "request to be transferred to

[1] *The Nation*, May 22, 2008. Reprinted with permission from the author and *The Nation*.

clerical duties at the Ministry of the Interior had been granted." Zen, of course, put in no such request.

Imagine Aurelio Zen as the Venetian cousin of Ian Rankin's John Rebus or Michael Connelly's Harry Bosch, someone resentful of the "shit for brains who carry the right party card" he has to flatter. Because he is morbidly haunted by the past, Zen is, by habit, a perpetual outsider wherever he ends up; even in his hometown, Venice, he tells a tourist, "I'm a stranger here myself." One can imagine the haunting organ score from Jean-Pierre Melville's *Le Samouraï* accompanying Zen as he drifts across the boot of Italy, his gaze "dull and opaque, like the surface of water where the last traces of some violent shock lingers on."

When we come across Zen in the first of Michael Dibdin's Zen novels, *Ratking* (1988), he is in limbo, a police commissioner attached to the Ministry of the Interior but permanently suspended from investigative duties, "nailed down, stuffed and varnished, with years of dreary routine to go before they would let him retire." His hangover from the *anni di piombo*—the so-called "years of lead," the era of escalating right- and left-wing violence in Italy—hasn't quite passed. He is long separated from his wife (though divorce seems elusive), living with his mother and having an affair with an American divorcée. The nearest he gets to real police work is "smashing the great stolen-toilet-roll racket at the Questura in Campobasso." But in *Ratking*, thanks to his expertise in kidnapping and a boost from a back-room political fix, he is dusted off and temporarily reassigned to investigate the snatching of a well-connected industrialist in Perugia. By the end of the novel Zen has managed to climb his way back into favor: he is promoted to *vice-questore* and reinstated on the active roster of the Polizia Criminale (Criminalpol). Throughout the case, however, he senses that "he was no more than a pawn in whatever sophisticated games were being played." In Zen's second adventure,

Vendetta (1990), his superiors assign him to investigate a mass murder in Sardinia; in reality, they send him there to solve nothing, only to create the pretense of police interest in the case. What they really want is for him to make sure that a leading Christian Democratic player avoids the dragnet.

This pattern repeats itself a number of times in the series. Zen will find himself in a position of assumed authority and influence, only to learn that he's a figurehead who is expected to conform to the wishes of his political bosses in Rome or turn a blind eye to whatever malfeasance has paralyzed the local Questura. Zen is reconciled to this imposture. But as cooperative as he is with his masters, and as keen as he is to work the system, his formidable skills as a gumshoe and his innate sense of justice always land him in trouble. Still, he manages to survive, thanks to his prowess and luck. At the end of *Vendetta*, in a grotesquely emblematic moment, Zen is summoned to the portal of true power in Italy, the Palazzo Sisti, the veritable Mount Olympus of the Christian Democratic Party. There, for services rendered, its chief member of Parliament (modeled undoubtedly on Giulio Andreotti, who enjoyed seven stints as Italy's prime minister) says to him, euphemistically, "If there's ever anything you need . . ." This, Zen muses, is "better than money in the bank!" At the time—the setting is the late 1980s—the Christian Democrats' power seemed as eternal as the city in which it was quartered. But it was a bargain only as lasting as Christian Democracy's hold on the summit of Italian society, which, as it turned out, was about to disintegrate.

When Dibdin started writing the Zen series, no one, let alone Dibdin, could have anticipated the seismic convulsions that would upend the Italian state; among the wreckage was the Christian Democratic Party, which dissolved in late 1993. The convulsions were triggered by the nationwide corruption investigations known as *Mani pulite* (Clean hands), which implicated almost all of Italy's political class, including key Christian

Democrats and their Socialist allies, but they were enabled too by the end of the cold war. Dibdin, not unlike Zen, seems to have been in the right place at the right time. His Zen series—eleven novels published between 1988 and 2007—covers a period when the politicians running the post-Christian Democratic Italian republic attempted to impose a consensus on Italian society, something the rulers of Italy have struggled and singularly failed to do since 1860, as historian John Foot has observed. Silvio Berlusconi, the head of Forza Italia, home of many former Christian Democrats, is the most vulgar and brash example of this new breed of politician—and there are more where he comes from, on the left and the right. They have attempted, quite successfully in some respects, to wipe from the historical databanks decades of civil war and political violence and to reconstruct Italy into a country like any other: a less politicized realm where a consumer culture rules. In its own way, Dibdin's Zen series sounds a melancholy note for the old Italy that seems to be disappearing before Zen's eyes. Dibdin seems to share a sentiment expressed by Peter Robb in the new postscript to his classic *Midnight in Sicily* (1996). After surveying the kidnappings, car bombings and political bosses that have scarred Italy, past and present, Robb writes, "In the brave new Italy of the two thousands, to look back at the Italy and Sicily of the second half of the twentieth century . . . arouses a kind of nostalgia . . . Beside Silvio Berlusconi . . . Giulio Andreotti has acquired a patina of antique probity, deeply respectful of the laws of the church and republic, austerely dedicated to party and career, and very, very careful with words."

Zen stalks the new Italy like a phantom, seeking out and bonding with fellow phantoms, people not afflicted by the amnesia that has fallen over Italy. In the extraordinarily eerie *Medusa* (2003), Zen meets one of these fellow phantoms, a burned-out and reclusive leftist journalist who broods on the *misteri d'Italia*, that secret network of events that has tainted Italy's recent history. The journalist says, "I can get by on my pension, more or less, so I've decided to devote my remaining years to writing a book."

"What about?" Zen asks.

"A definitive account, explanation and analysis of all the *misteri d'Italia*."

"A slim volume, then," commented Zen.

"Virtually invisible."

The murders in the book are traced by Zen to a clandestine military organization named Medusa, created in the 1970s as a secret extralegal operation to combat the Italian far left. *Medusa* burrows into the occult history of the period, but it's clear that no one really wants to know about the *misteri d'Italia*. "The truth," Zen's friend tells him, "is that no one cares about all that stuff anymore." Zen comes across a local commune that reeks of "frustration, even despair, as unmistakable as mould." History is now what was on television last night; 1978 might as well be 1878. Even the novel's villain—another of Zen's fellow phantoms—pines for a former political opponent: "He was our sworn enemy thirty years ago, of course, like all the PCI crowd, but times have changed. When I see the shallow consumerist trash running around these days I almost begin to feel nostalgic for enemies like that."

A similar sense of nostalgia might be warranted for Michael Dibdin, who died suddenly last year after a short illness. He was 60. The British press devoted significant space to recapping Dibdin's career. The *Guardian* took the unusual step—for the death of a mystery writer, at least—of lamenting Dibdin's passing in a lead editorial, singling out the Zen series: "There can be little argument that Silvio Berlusconi has been the prime mover in compelling the modern generation of British middle-class visitors to view Italy and Italians in a less romantically indulgent light than many were previously inclined to do. But

Aurelio Zen played a very important part too . . . The melancholy detective created by the late Michael Dibdin lifted the curtain on a much more sinister Italy than the EM Forster version that had inspired generations of starry-eyed visitors from the north."

Dibdin, by most accounts, lived as peripatetic an existence as his creation Zen. His journeying included a childhood in Ulster; education in Sussex, England, and Alberta, Canada; a stint teaching at the University of Perugia (which must have initiated him into the vagaries of Italian bureaucracy); and then, these last dozen years, a life in Seattle.

I remember seeing him skulking around Oxford in the early 1990s. One evening, in a pub, some friends and I were discussing Dibdin's latest novel, the merciless, wickedly funny *Dirty Tricks*, about sleazy English language-instruction schools in Oxford (Dibdin wrote seven non-Zen crime novels, of which *Dirty Tricks* was the finest). Somehow we all seemed to recognize ourselves in the novel, to the extent that each of us recounted a scene that we insisted Dibdin must have based on us. This fantasizing reached a lurid pitch when one of us claimed to have been the inspiration for a sex scene involving a couch. It was at this moment that I turned to see Dibdin sitting beside us. His face resembled the visage he had given to Zen: "expressionless as the frescoed image of some minor saint who was being martyred in some unspeakable way but, thanks to his steadfast faith, remained at peace with himself."

In the United States, the quality of Dibdin's novels has long been celebrated in the ghetto of the crime fiction round-up pages of our newspapers. In a short review in the *Wall Street Journal* of Dibdin's last novel, *End Games* (2007), you can almost hear the reviewer weep for lack of space as he quickly catalogs canonical authors to define Dibdin's prowess: "[Dibdin] evokes not so much the terse action scenes of hard-boiled masters as the word-drunk prose of such language-besotted authors as Anthony Burgess, Vladimir Nabokov and Lawrence Durrell . . . The next time you hear a snob speak condescendingly of the detective story, tell them to go take a hike—or to read a Dibdin novel."

Dibdin could never have been mistaken for a literary novelist slumming in the genre. He was an extremely cultured, extremely serious crime novelist. His novels resembled the "hard novels" of Georges Simenon and the dark, subtle paranoias of Leonardo Sciascia's crime stories, but they also crackle with the fun, puzzles and escapism of Conan Doyle. In *Back to Bologna* (2005) and *Così Fan Tutti* (1996), the humor is so riotous and operatic that one almost misses the melancholy beauty and atmosphere of novels like *Dead Lagoon* (1994), whose portrayal of Venice merits comparison with Jan Morris.

End Games is Southern gothic, Italian style. It opens with what appears to be a form of ritualistic murder. A man dressed "like a corpse" visits a church in the local countryside, then visits the ruins of an old stately home, where he seems to bless himself—after which his head is blown off by a remote-controlled device. "Calabria," as one character observes, "can be harsh to her sons." Zen has been temporarily transferred to the region to cover for the police chief of Cosenza, who is recovering from a wound to his foot that he suffered while cleaning his pistol. Zen, of course, is a mere figurehead. His new colleagues tell him that he has no need to concern himself with the day-to-day workings of police headquarters. Zen is happy to oblige them; he is left alone to grumble about the proliferation of tomatoes in the local diet and the volatile local weather.

Zen's grumblings acquire a different flavor when Peter Newman, an American lawyer scouting locations for a film company, is kidnapped. The missing lawyer, it turns out, is actually a Calabrian, the scion of a much-hated feudal family that had ruled the local area as its fief until the end of World War II. When Newman's headless corpse is discovered, Zen, an old hand when it comes to kidnappings, is confounded. Why, he wonders, would a kidnap gang "destroy a potentially very profitable piece of merchandise without even putting it on the market?" Zen's process of discovery involves, in some respect, the recovery of his vocation. It also returns him to the parallel world of Italy's secret state that he first encountered in 1978. But his sleuthing takes him further into the past, to the repressive old southern *latifondo* system of estate farming, the Fascist era and its immediate aftermath. With its legacies of ghastly aristocratic violence, old ruins and a changeling, *End Games* is partly a gothic revenge drama, where memories, certainly in this part of Calabria, can linger like unexploded ordnance. Zen senses that to live in Calabria is to inhabit several eras simultaneously. The trashy world of Italia-lite that seems to have drained Italy of its substance has stopped at Cosenza: "For every ten kilometres you travelled between Rome and Cosenza, you moved back another year into the past, finally arriving in the mid-1950s. Authenticity was not as yet under serious threat here, and in some way that he couldn't have explained, that slewed the ethical equations too. What would have been good enough elsewhere simply wouldn't do here, back in the lost realm of the real."

But in "the lost realm of the real comes violence, clan ritual and death." "Life is an acquired taste, Signor Zen, but death has mass-market appeal," a former spook tells him. Dibdin's rendering of the terrible violence and *tristesse* of the region, the "sense of generalised and ineradicable sadness about the place, despite its natural beauty," is beguiling, the trait that makes his mysteries so distinctive. Dibdin has always been at his most pungent when writing about the Mezzogiorno. In *Blood Rain* (1999), he evoked the bleak interior towns, dead villages and holy terrors of Sicily with a sulfuric intensity that rivals Sciascia's in *The Day of the Owl* and *To Each His Own*. He also captured the sense of generalized apathy and the tragic fate of those who choose action over resignation. While *End Games* never has the same tragic pitch as *Blood Rain*, it reminds you what a fine and rare vintage Dibdin is. *End Games* is marred only by a slightly irritating subplot involving a scam by Peter Newman's former colleagues, which involves looting Cosenza of the mythical treasures of King Alaric. This reads like a cut-and-paste from a Donald Westlake caper like *The Hot Rock* or *Kahawa*.

It's strange to read Dibdin's last novel with a sense of nostalgia, but the realization that we will see neither Dibdin nor Zen again shadows one's expectations of *End Games*. One winces as the novel closes with Zen sitting in one of those soullessly elongated regional train stations that dot Italy, waiting for the train, to return to Rome. One struggles to stifle the sadistic wish that Dibdin had been clairvoyant enough about his own passing to kill off Zen in *End Games*. (In *Blood Rain* he sort of does that, but, as with Conan Doyle's greatest creation, he brings Zen back in *And Then You Die*.) One of the most memorable scenes in the novel is when a sleazy, disbarred lawyer—the fixer who arranged for Newman's kidnapping—reminds Zen that in Calabria life is lived in the subjunctive. Likewise, it is our fate to wonder what might have been and to approach *End Games* in the subjunctive mood.

More than a decade ago, Dibdin edited *The Vintage Book of Classic Crime* (originally published as *The Picador Book of Crime Writing* in Britain), a robust, wide-ranging but eclectic anthology of mostly Anglo-American crime writing. Each section of the book featured a short, erudite essay by Dibdin about an aspect of the genre. These little essays not only explored the varietals; they illuminated Dibdin's experience as a practitioner. Suggestively, he argued that the best crime writing is "eccentric—the product of a creative struggle against the overwhelmingly centripetal force of the genre." He could have been describing his own work, of course: short, terse, sometimes rather compressed novels that rarely ran more than 250 pages.

But within these parameters, Dibdin was a playful novelist who gave the impression that he didn't want to get bored or locked down by the genre. His crime stories blended the straightforward and counterintuitive, variations on noir, *giallo*, revenge tragedy, conspiracy thriller—though never, interestingly enough, descending into the abyss of Borgesian paranoia that energized Sciascia's *One Way or Another* and *Equal Danger.* But the peculiar qualities that Dibdin observed about the Swedish husband-and-wife crime-writing team of Maj Sjöwall and Per Wahlöö summarize the brooding beauty of his own work: the duo "transcends the level of the average police procedural thanks to a prevailing sense of unease which in the end seems as much existential as ideological."

The odd thing about *The Vintage Book of Classic Crime* is that only two Italian writers are included, neither of whom is Leonardo Sciascia. Neither is an example of crime fiction either; rather, they are examples of genre criticism by Umberto Eco ("The basic question of philosophy . . . is the same as that of the detective novel: who is guilty?") and Antonio Gramsci (a few gemlike paragraphs from the *Prison Notebooks* where he favors Chesterton over Conan Doyle for his intuitive rather than rationalist approach to detection). Sciascia is an obvious influence on Dibdin's work—especially *Cabal* (1992), for which Sciascia provides the epigraph—and the absence of him and Carlo Emilio Gadda, author of the classic *That Awful Mess on Via Merulana*, is a paradox. (Some of Sciascia's and Gadda's novels are available in new editions from New York Review Books.) The anthology was published at a time when, according to one observer, Alan Taylor in *Scotland on Sunday*, "it feels as if there are more expatriate thriller writers in Italy than there are Italian ice-cream parlours in Britain. Italians—with the honourable exception of the Sicilian Leonardo Sciascia—generally don't write whodunnits, leaving them to the likes of Magdalen Nabb, Donna Leon and Michael Dibdin."

Coincidentally, since the publication of Dibdin's anthology, a number of Italian crime novelists have come to the fore, thanks in part to a steady trickle of translation from small presses like Bitter Lemon and Europa. In fact, the blurb on an excellent recent anthology, *Crimini*, boasts that Italian crime fiction is enjoying a renaissance, "replacing that of Scandinavia as the fastest growing in the genre." Probably the most palatable to the middlebrow palate are the Sicilian novelist Andrea Camilleri's genial Inspector Montalbano novels, but the most striking offer tough, more cynical fare: writers like Niccolò Ammaniti, Gianrico Carofiglio, Massimo Carlotto and Giuseppe Genna, whose novels (Carlotto's and Genna's, particularly) percolate with a dark, sleazy energy and growl with the lament of a Paolo Conte song and lost political dreams. Genna's *In the Name of Ishmael* is probably the most paranoid conspiracy thriller to see print; its featured psycho killer is a former US Secretary of State familiar to readers of this magazine.

If there's one writer who ratifies Dibdin's dark, ironic but oddly nostalgic vision, it is Carlo Lucarelli. Lucarelli, a well-known TV personality in Italy, hosts a late-night show devoted to unsolved mysteries, whose subjects range from the mysterious death of the Italian industrialist Enrico Mattei to the murder of Pier Paolo Pasolini. Lucarelli came to attention in Italy in 1990 with *Carte Blanche*, the first of a brilliant trilogy of very short novels set in a period stretching from the collapse of Mussolini's Salo Republic, a puppet regime of the Nazis that ruled Northern Italy from 1943 to 1945, to the earlier years of the postwar Italian Republic. They feature Commissario De Luca, a weary detective and former member of Mussolini's political police who, as *Carte Blanche* begins, has transferred back to the ordinary force just as he realizes that the Salo Republic is about to collapse. Wracked by bad conscience and a lack of sleep, he tries to claw back his professional pride as an ordinary homicide detective. Unfortunately, the first homicide he has to investigate involves a victim with strong connections to the Fascist elite. For a novel of such slender size (a mere 120 pages), *Carte Blanche* is a richly atmospheric *policier* that, reeking of the decay and political squalor of the late Mussolini period, recalls Bertolucci's *Il Conformista* and Hammett's *Red Harvest*.

The nasty atmospherics continue in *The Damned Season*, a claustrophobic and nervy thriller set in the month after Italy's liberation from fascism. De Luca is posing as an engineer in the countryside between Bologna and Rome, fearful that he is on a partisan hit list. After inadvertently divulging his identity, he is blackmailed into heading a homicide investigation—one that finds him ensnared in the rivalries of competing partisan factions. The trilogy's final novel, *Villa Delle Oche*, is set during the days leading up to the contentious first election after the liberation, in April 1948, where De Luca is working for the Bologna vice squad. Still sleepless, he is also guilt-ridden by former associations and has developed a nervous tic of chewing the inside of his cheek while on the trail of a murderer who seems to have dispatched several lowlifes who have Communist sympathies. It is a bitter, ironic novel that closes an era when everything seemed politically possible in Italy, and whose nippy pace is enlivened by the use of hysterical contemporary newspaper headlines and political slogans, including this priceless one: "If the Christian Democrats win all of Italy will be a seminary: No more Charlie Chaplin, Totò, or Rita Hayworth. You'll die of boredom."

There's a slightly demented, baroque quality to Lucarelli's novels reminiscent of Italian horror director Dario Argento. Any writer of Lucarelli's generation cannot approach the crime thriller without wrestling with the achievement of the cinematic master of the Italian *giallo*. The two other novels of Lucarelli's that have been translated into English, *Almost Blue* and *Day After Day*, have a similar staccato-like pulse that bares the imprint of Argento's *Deep Red.* Their protagonist, a sultry young Southerner, Inspector Grazia Negro, is as finely realized a character as Aurelio Zen, a cop who has the dual burden of hunting serial killers and professional killers and combating her boorish male colleagues. Of the two novels, *Almost Blue* is the superior, a sublime, sinewy work that is icy, elegant and swathed in darkness. It is dominated by two obsessive narrators: one, a serial killer filled with self-loathing; the other, a blind recluse named Simone who spends insomniac nights listening to the police radio and following the movement of Inspector Negro. Simone can never see Bologna, but his imagined city—woven from the lonely nights listening to police radio—sparkles like a magic lantern. His voice is eerie, elegiac and mostly what makes *Almost Blue* such a memorable novel. Colors have a different meaning for him. "For me, a pretty girl might have blonde hair, but a truly beautiful girl would be *b*arefoot, *b*rave and have *blue* hair."

It's as if Negro, De Luca and Zen are neighbors whose homes are haunted by the same ghosts—phantoms that Lucarelli and Dibdin want to bring back to life. It's a lonely and bitter task, especially in light of what Geoff Andrews has called "Italy's hour of darkness": Berlusconi's "third coming" and the radical left's liquidation in Italy's recent elections. "If we want things to stay as they are, things will have to change," Tancredi tells his uncle in Lampedusa's *The Leopard.* Dibdin's and Lucarelli's stories about the *misteri d'Italia* are poignant and distressing confirmations of those dark words.

Fiction

FROM *TOTAL CHAOS*
By Jean-Claude Izzo

Translated from the French
by Howard Curtis

PROLOGUE
RUE DES PISTOLES, TWENTY YEARS AFTER

All he had was her address. Rue des Pistoles, in the old neighborhood. It was years since he'd last been in Marseilles. But he didn't have a choice. Not now.

It was June 2nd, and it was raining. Despite the rain, the taxi driver refused to turn into the back alleys. He dropped him in front of Montée-des-Accoules. More than a hundred steps to climb and a maze of streets between there and Rue des Pistoles. The ground was littered with garbage sacks spilling their contents. There was a pungent smell on the streets, a mixture of piss, dampness and mildew. The only big change was that even this neighborhood was being redeveloped. Some houses had been demolished, others had had their fronts repainted ocher and pink, with Italian-style green and blue shutters.

Even on Rue des Pistoles, maybe one of the narrowest streets of all, only one side, the side with even-numbered houses, was still standing. The other side had been razed to the ground, as had the houses on Rue Rodillat, and in their place was a parking lot. That was the first thing he saw when he turned the corner from Rue du Refuge. The developers seemed to have taken a breather here. The houses were blackened and dilapidated, eaten away by sewer vegetation.

He was too early, he knew. But he didn't want to go to a bistro and sit drinking one coffee after another, looking at his watch, waiting for a reasonable hour to wake Lole. What he wanted was to have his coffee sitting comfortably in a real apartment. He hadn't done that for months. As soon as she opened the door, he headed straight for the only armchair in the room, as if it was something he'd often done. He stroked the armrest with his hand, sat down slowly, and closed his eyes. It was only afterwards that he finally looked at her. Twenty years after.

She was standing. Bolt upright, as always. Her hands deep in the pockets of a straw-colored bathrobe. The color made her skin look browner than usual and emphasized the blackness of her hair, which she was wearing short now. Her hips may have grown thicker, he wasn't sure. She'd become a woman, but she hadn't changed. Lole, the Gypsy. She'd always been beautiful.

"I could use a coffee."

She nodded. Without a word. Without a smile. He'd dragged her from her sleep. Maybe from a dream in which she and Manu were hotfooting it down to Seville, not a care in the world, their pockets bulging with cash. She probably had that dream every night. But Manu was dead. He'd been dead three months.

He sprawled in the armchair, stretching his legs. Then he lit a cigarette. The best in a long time, no question.

"I was expecting you." Lole handed him a cup. "But not this early."

"I took a night train. A train full of legionnaires. Fewer checks. Safer."

She was staring off into the air. Wherever Manu was.

"Aren't you going to sit down?"

"I drink my coffee standing up."

"You still don't have a phone."

"No."

She smiled. For a moment, the sleep seemed to vanish from her face. She'd dismissed the dream. She looked at him with melancholy eyes. He was tired, and anxious. His old fears. He liked the fact that Lole didn't say much, didn't feel the need to explain. It was a way of getting their lives back in order. Once and for all.

There was a smell of mint in the room. He looked around. It was a big room, with unadorned white walls. No shelves, no knick-knacks or books. Furniture reduced to the bare essentials. A table, chairs, and a sideboard that didn't match, and a single bed over by the window. A door led to another room, the bedroom. From where he was, he could see part of the bed. Rumpled blue sheets. He'd forgotten the night smells. The smell of bodies. Lole's smell. When they made love, her armpits smelled of basil. His eyes were starting to close. He looked again at the bed near the window.

"You could sleep there."

"I'd like to sleep now."

Later, he saw her walking across the room. He didn't know how long he'd slept. To see the time on his watch, he'd have had to move, and he didn't want to move. He preferred to watch Lole coming and going through half-closed eyes.

She'd come out of the bathroom wrapped in a terry towel. She wasn't very big. But she had everything she needed, and in the right places too. And she had gorgeous legs. Then he'd fallen asleep again. His fears had vanished.

It had gotten dark. Lole was wearing a sleeveless black dress. Simple, but it really suited her, hugged her body nicely. He looked at her legs again. This time she felt his eyes on her.

"I'm leaving you the keys. There's coffee heating. I made some more."

She was saying only the most obvious things, avoiding everything else. He sat up, and took out a cigarette, his eyes still on her.

"I'll be back late. Don't wait up for me."

"Are you still a bar girl?"

"Hostess. At the Vamping. I don't want to see you hanging around there."

He remembered the Vamping, overlooking the Catalan beach. Amazing decor, like something out of a Scorsese movie. The singer and the band behind stands full of spangles. Tangos, boleros, cha-chas, mambos, that kind of thing.

"I wasn't planning to."

She shrugged. "I've never been sure what you were planning." Her smile made clear she wasn't expecting a reply. "Are you going to see Fabio?"

He'd thought she'd ask him that. He'd asked himself the same thing. But he'd dismissed the idea. Fabio was a cop. That had drawn a bit of a line under their youth, their friendship. He'd have liked to see Fabio again, though.

"Later. Maybe. How is he?"

"The same. Like us. Like you, like Manu. Lost. None of us have known what to do with our lives. Cop or robber, it makes no difference..."

"You liked him a lot, didn't you?"

"Yes, I liked him a lot."

He felt a pang in his heart. "Have you seen him again?"

"Not in the last three months." She picked up her bag and a white linen jacket. He still hadn't taken his eyes off her.

"Under your pillow," she said at last, and it was clear from her face that his surprise amused her. "The rest is in the sideboard drawer."

And with that, she left. He lifted the pillow. The 9mm was there. He'd sent it to Lole, in an express package, before he left Paris. The subways and railroad stations were swarming with cops. The French Republic had decided it wanted to be whiter than white. Zero immigration. The new French dream. There might be checks, and he didn't want any hassle. Not that kind. Having false papers was bad enough.

The gun. A present from Manu, for his twentieth birthday.

Even then, Manu had been a bit crazy. He'd never parted with it, but he'd never used it either. You didn't kill someone like that. Even when you were threatened. That had happened to him a few times, in different places. There was always another solution. That was what he thought. And he was still alive. But today, he needed it. To kill a man.

It was just after eight. The rain had stopped, and the warm air hit him in the face as he left the building. He'd taken a long shower and put on a pair of black cotton pants, a black polo shirt, and a denim jacket. He'd put his mocassins back on, without socks. He turned into Rue du Panier.

This was his neighborhood. He was born here. Rue des Petits-Puits, two streets along from where Pierre Puget was born. His father had lived on Rue de la Charité when he first arrived in France, fleeing poverty and Mussolini. He was twenty, and had two of his brothers in tow. *Nabos*—Neapolitans. Three others had gone to Argentina. They did the jobs the French wouldn't touch. His father was hired as a longshoreman, paid by the centime. "Harbor dogs," they were called—it was meant as an insult. His mother worked packing dates, fourteen hours a day. In the evenings, the *nabos* and the people from the North, the *babis*, met up on the streets. They pulled chairs out in front of their doors, talked through the windows. Just like in Italy. Just like the good old days.

He hadn't recognized his house. That had been redeveloped, too. He'd walked on past. Manu was from Rue Baussenque. A dark, damp building, where his mother, already pregnant with him, moved in with two of her brothers. His father, José Manuel, had been shot by Franco's men. Immigrants, exiles, they all arrived full of hope. By the time Lole appeared on the scene, with her family, Manu and he were already grown up. Sixteen. At least, that's what they told the girls.

Living in the Panier wasn't something you boasted about.

Ever since the nineteenth century it had been a neighborhood of sailors and whores. A blight on the city. One big brothel. For the Nazis, who'd dreamed of destroying it, it was a *source of degeneration for the Western world.* His father and mother had lived through the humiliation. Ordered to leave in the middle of the night. January 24th 1943. Twenty thousand people. Finding a wheelbarrow quickly, loading a few possessions. Mistreated by the French gendarmes and mocked by the German soldiers. Pushing the wheelbarrow along the Canebière at daybreak, watched by people on their way to work. At school, the other kids pointed the finger at them. Even working class kids, from Belle de Mai. But not for long. They simply broke their fingers! He and Manu knew their bodies and clothes smelled of mildew. The smell of the neighborhood. The first girl he'd ever kissed had that smell at the back of her throat. But they didn't give a damn. They loved life. They were good looking. And they knew how to fight.

He turned onto Rue du Refuge, to walk back down. Some distance away, six Arab kids, aged between fourteen and seventeen, stood talking, next to a gleaming new moped. They watched him coming, warily. A new face in the neighborhood spelled danger. A cop. An informer. Or the new owner of a renovated building, who'd go to the town hall and complain about the lack of security. The cops would come and check them out. Take them down to the station. Maybe rough them up. Hassle them. When he drew level with the kids, he gave the one who seemed to be the leader a short, sharp look, then walked on. Nobody moved. They'd understood each other.

He crossed Place de Lenche, which was deserted, then walked down toward the harbor. He stopped at the first phone booth. Batisti answered.

"I'm Manu's friend."

"Hi, pal. Come by tomorrow, have a drink. About one, at the Péano. It'll be great to meet. See you, kid."

He hung up. A man of few words, Batisti. No time to tell him he'd rather have gone anywhere but there. Anywhere but the Péano. It was the bar where the painters went. Ambrogiani had showed his first canvases there. Then others had come along, influenced by him. Poor imitations, some of them. But journalists went there, too. From right across the political spectrum. *Le Provençal, La Marseillaise, Agence France Presse, Libération. Pastis* knocked down the barriers between them. At night, they waited till the papers were put to sleep, then went into the back room to listen to jazz. Both Petruccianis had played there, father and son. With Aldo Romano. There'd been so many nights. Nights of trying to figure out what his life was all about. That night, Harry was at the piano.

"All you need to figure out is what you want," Lole said.

"Yeah. And what I want right now is a change of scenery."

Manu had come back with the umpteenth round. After midnight, they stopped counting. Three scotches, doubles. He'd sat down and raised his glass, smiling beneath his moustache.

"Cheers, lovebirds."

"Shut up, you," Lole had said.

He stared at the two of you as if you were strange animals, then turned his back on you and concentrated on the music. Lole was looking at you. You'd emptied your glass. Slowly. Deliberately. Your mind was made up. You were leaving. You stood up and went out, unsteady on your feet. You were leaving. You left. Without saying a word to Manu, the only friend you still had. Without saying a word to Lole, who'd just turned twenty. Who you loved. Who you both loved. Cairo, Djibouti, Aden, Harar. The itinerary of an eternal adolescent. That was before you lost your innocence. From Argentina to Mexico. Ending up in Asia, to get rid of your remaining illusions. And an international arrest warrant on your ass, for trafficking in works of art.

You were back in Marseilles because of Manu. To take out the son of a bitch who'd killed him. He'd been coming out of Chez Félix, a bistrot on Rue Caisserie where he liked to have lunch. Lole was waiting for him in Madrid, at her mother's place. He was about to come into a tidy bit of cash. For a break-in that had gone without a hitch, at a big Marseilles lawyer's, Eric Brunel, on Boulevard Longchamp. They'd decided to go to Seville. To forget Marseilles and the hard times.

You weren't after the guy who'd whacked Manu. A hitman, for sure. Cold and anonymous. Someone from Lyons, or Milan. Someone you wouldn't find. The guy you were after was the scumbag who'd ordered the hit. Who'd wanted Manu killed. You didn't want to know why. You didn't need any reasons. Not a single one. Anyone attacked Manu, it was like they'd attacked you.

The sun woke him. Nine o'clock. He lay there on his back, and smoked his first cigarette. He hadn't slept so deeply in months. He always dreamed that he was sleeping somewhere other than where he was. A brothel in Harar. A Tijuana jail. On the Rome-Paris express. Anywhere. But always somewhere else. During the night, he'd dreamed he was sleeping at Lole's place. And that's where he really was. It was as if he'd come home. He smiled. He'd barely heard her come back and close the door of her bedroom. She was sleeping in her blue sheets, rebuilding her broken dream. There was still a piece missing. Manu. Unless it was him. But he'd long ago rejected that idea. That would have been to put himself in too good a light. Twenty years was a hell of a long time to mourn.

He stood up, made coffee, and took a shower. The water was hot. He felt much better. He closed his eyes, and imagined Lole coming to join him. Just like before. Clinging to his body. Her pussy against his dick. Her hands gliding over his back, his buttocks. He started to get a hard-on. He turned on the cold water, and screamed.

Lole put on a record. *Pura salsa.* One of Azuquita's first recordings. Her tastes hadn't changed. He attempted a few dance steps, which made her smile. She moved forward to kiss him. As she did so, he caught a glimpse of her breasts. Like pears waiting to be picked. He didn't look away quickly enough. Their eyes met. She froze, pulled the belt of her bathrobe tighter, and went into the kitchen. He felt wretched. An eternity passed. She came back with two cups of coffee.

"A guy asked after you last night. Wanted to know if you were around. A friend of yours. Malabe. Frankie Malabe."

He didn't know any Malabe. A cop? More likely an informer. He didn't like them approaching Lole. But at the same time it reassured him. The Customs cops knew he was back in France, but not where. Not yet. They were angling for leads. He still needed a bit of time. Two days maybe. Everything depended on what Batisti had to sell.

"Why are you here?"

He picked up his jacket. Don't answer, he told himself. Don't get involved in a question and answer session. He wouldn't be able to lie to her, and he wouldn't be able to tell her what he was going to do. Not now. But he had to do it. Just as, one day, he'd had to leave. He'd never been able to answer her questions. There were no answers, only questions. That was the only thing he'd learned in life. It wasn't much, but it was more certain than believing in God.

"Forget I asked." Behind him, she opened the door. "Not asking questions has never gotten me anywhere."

The two-storey parking garage on Cours d'Estienne d'Orves had finally been demolished, and what had once been the prison canal was now a lovely square. The houses had been restored, the fronts repainted, the ground paved. An Italian style square. The bars and restaurants all had terraces, with white tables and parasols. People wanted to be seen, just like in

Italy. The only thing missing was elegance. The Péano also had its terrace, which was already full. Young people mostly. Very clean-cut. The interior had been refurbished. The decor was hip but cold. The paintings had been replaced by crappy reproductions. But he almost preferred it this way. It helped him keep the memories at arm's length.

He sat down at the bar and ordered a *pastis*. In the room, there was a couple who looked to him like a hooker and her pimp. He might be wrong, of course. Although they were talking in low voices, their discussion seemed rather animated. He leaned an elbow on the brand new zinc counter and watched the front door.

The minutes passed. Nobody came in. He ordered another *pastis*. He heard the words "Son of a bitch!" followed by a sharp sound. Eyes turned to the couple. Silence. The woman ran out. The man stood up, left a fifty-franc bill, and went out after her.

On the terrace, a man folded the newspaper he'd been reading. He was in his sixties. A sailor's cap on his head. Blue cotton pants, a white short-sleeved shirt over the pants. Blue espadrilles. He stood up and came toward him. Batisti.

He spent the afternoon staking out the place. Monsieur Charles, as he was known in the underworld, lived in one of the opulent villas overlooking the Corniche. Amazing villas, some with pinnacles, others with columns. Gardens full of palms, oleanders and fig trees. After the Roucas Blanc, the road winds across the little hill, a crisscross of lanes, some of them barely tarred. He had taken the bus, a no. 55, as far as Place des Pilotes, at the top of the last slope. Then he'd continued on foot.

He could see out over the harbor. The whole sweep of it from L'Estaque to Pointe-Rouge, with the Frioul islands and the Château d'If. Marseilles in Cinemascope. Beautiful. He started on the downward slope, facing the sea. He was only two villas away from Zucca's villa. He looked at his watch. Four fifty-eight. The gates of the villa opened. A black Mercedes appeared, and parked. He walked past the villa, and the Mercedes, and continued as far as Rue des Espérettes, which cuts across the Roucas Blanc. He crossed the street. Another ten paces, and he'd reach the bus stop. According to the schedules, the 55 passed at 5:05. He leaned against the stop, looked at his watch, and waited.

The Mercedes reversed along the curb, and stopped. Two men inside, including the driver. Zucca appeared. He must have been about seventy. Elegantly dressed, like all these old gangsters. He even had a straw hat, and a white poodle on a leash. Preceded by the dog, he walked down as far as the crossing on Rue des Espérettes. He stopped. The bus was coming. Zucca crossed to the shady side of the street, then came down the Roucas Blanc. He passed the bus stop. The Mercedes set off, at a snail's pace.

Batisti's information had been worth the fifty thousand francs he'd paid. It was all there in writing, without a single detail missing. Zucca took the same walk every day, except Sunday, when his family visited with him. At six o'clock, the Mercedes drove him back to the villa. But Batisti didn't know why Zucca had gone after Manu. He'd gotten no farther toward understanding that. There had to be a connection with the break-in at the lawyer's. That was what he was starting to think. But the truth was, he didn't give a damn. All he was interested in was Zucca. Monsieur Charles.

He hated these old gangsters. On intimate terms with the cops and the judges. Never done time. Thought they were better than anyone else. Zucca had a face like Brando in *The Godfather*. They all had faces like that. Here, in Palermo, in Chicago. Everywhere you went. And now he had one of them in his sights. He was going to take one of them out. For friendship's sake. And to give vent to his hatred.

He was looking through Lole's things. The chest, the closets. He'd come back slightly drunk. He wasn't searching for anything in particular, just looking, thinking maybe he'd uncover a secret. About Lole, about Manu. But there was nothing to uncover. Life had slipped through their fingers, faster than money.

In a drawer, he found a whole bunch of photos. That was all they had left. He was disappointed. He almost threw everything in the trashcan. But there were these three photos. The same photo taken three times. Same time, same place. Manu and him. Lole and Manu. Lole and him. It was at the end of the big pier, behind the commercial port. To get there, they'd had to slip past the guards. We were good at that, he thought. Behind them, the city. In the background, the islands. The three of you came out of the water, breathless and happy. You feasted your eyes on boats leaving in the setting sun. Lole read aloud from *Exile* by Saint-John Perse. *The wind's militias in the sands of exile.* On the way back, you took Lole's hand. You dared to do that. Manu never had.

That night, you left Manu at the Bar du Lenche. Everything had turned upside down. No more laughter. None of you had spoken. You'd all drunk *pastis* in embarrassed silence. Desire had distanced you from Manu. The next day, you had to go pick him up from the station house. He'd spent the night there. For starting a fight with two legionnaires. His right eye wouldn't open. He had a cut lip. Bruises everywhere.

"I got two of them! I really did!"

Lole kissed him on the forehead. He hugged her and started sobbing.

"Fuck," he said. "This is hard."

And he fell asleep, just like that, on Lole's lap.

Lole woke him at ten o'clock. He'd slept soundly, but his tongue felt furred. The smell of coffee pervaded the room. Lole sat down on the edge of the bed. Her hand brushed his shoulder. Her lips rested on his forehead, then on his lips. A furtive, tender kiss. If happiness existed, he'd just come close to it.

"I'd forgotten."

"If that's true, get out of here right now!"

She handed him a cup of coffee, and stood up to get hers. She was smiling and happy. As if the sadness hadn't yet reawakened.

"You don't want to sit down. Just like before."

"I prefer—"

"To have your coffee standing up, I know."

She smiled again. He couldn't get enough of her smile, her mouth. He clung to her eyes. They shone the way they had that night. You'd taken off her T-shirt, then your shirt. You'd pressed your bellies together and stayed like that without talking. Just breathing. Her eyes on you all the time.

"Don't ever leave me."

You'd promised.

But you'd left. Manu had stayed. And Lole had waited. But maybe Manu had stayed because someone needed to take care of Lole. And Lole hadn't followed you, because she'd thought it was unfair to abandon Manu. He'd started to think these things, since Manu died. Knowing he had to come back. And here he was. Marseilles had caught in his throat again. With Lole as an aftertaste.

Lole's eyes were shining more brightly. She was holding back the tears. She knew that something was going down. And that whatever it was would change her life. She'd had a premonition after Manu's funeral, during the hours she'd spent with Fabio. She could sense it now. She was good at sensing when something was going to happen. But she wouldn't say anything. It was up to him to speak.

He picked up the brown envelope he'd left beside the bed. "This is a ticket for Paris. The high speed train, 1:54 today. This is a checkroom ticket. The Gare de Lyon. Another one, for the

Gare Montparnasse. Two suitcases to be collected. In each one, there's a hundred thousand francs, hidden under a pile of old clothes. This postcard is from a very good restaurant at Port-Mer, near Cancale in Brittany. On the back, Marine's number. Get in touch with her. She can get you anything you want. Whatever she does for you, don't haggle over the price. I've booked a room for you at the Hotel des Marronniers, on Rue Jacob. Five nights, in your name. There'll be a letter for you at the reception desk."

She hadn't moved. She was frozen. Her eyes had gradually emptied of all expression. "Don't I get a word in edgewise?"

"No."

"Is that all you have to say?"

What he had to say would have taken ages, but he could have summed it up in a couple of sentences. I'm sorry. I love you. But they didn't have time for that anymore. Or rather, time had overtaken them. The future was behind them. Ahead, nothing but memories and regrets. He looked up at her, with as much detachment as he could muster.

"Close your bank account. Destroy your credit card. And your checkbook. Change identity as soon as possible. Marine will arrange that for you."

"And you?" she said with difficulty.

"I'll call you tomorrow morning."

He looked at his watch, and stood up. He passed close to her, averting his gaze, and went into the bathroom and locked the door behind him. He didn't want Lole to join him in the shower. He looked at his face in the mirror. He didn't like what he saw. He felt old. He'd forgotten how to smile. Bitter creases had appeared at the corners of his mouth, and they wouldn't go away. He wasn't yet forty-five and today was going to be the worst day of his life.

He heard the first guitar chord of *Entre dos aguas*. Paco de Lucia. Lole had turned the volume up. She was standing in front of the stereo with her arms folded, smoking a cigarette.

"You're getting nostalgic."

"Screw you."

He took the gun, loaded it, put on the safety, and wedged it between his shirt and the back of his pants. She'd turned around and was watching his every movement.

"Hurry up. I wouldn't want you to miss that train."

"What are you going to do?"

"Set the cat among the pigeons. I think."

The moped's engine was idling. It hadn't misfired once. Four fifty-one. Rue des Espérettes, just down the hill from Zucca's villa. It was hot. Sweat ran down his back. He wanted it to be over with.

He'd spent all morning looking for the Arab kids. They constantly changed streets. That was their rule. It probably served no purpose, but he supposed they had their reasons. He'd found them on Rue Fontaine-de-Caylus, which had become a square, with trees and benches. They were the only people there. Nobody from the neighborhood ever sat in the square. They preferred to stay by their front doors. The older kids were sitting on the steps of a house, while the younger ones were standing, the moped beside them. When the leader saw him coming, he'd stood up, and the others had moved aside.

"I need the bike. For the afternoon. Till six o'clock. Two thousand, cash."

He looked anxiously around. He'd counted on there being no one to catch the bus. If someone showed up, he'd let it go. If any passenger wanted to get off the bus, he wouldn't know until it was too late, but that was a risk he was prepared to take. Then he told himself that if he took that risk, he might as well take the other. He started calculating. The bus stops. The door opens. The passenger gets on. The bus starts off again. Four minutes. No, yesterday, it had taken only three minutes.

But let's say four. Zucca would have crossed by then. No, he would have seen the moped and let it pass. He emptied his head of all thoughts, counting the minutes over and over. Yes, it was possible. But after that, the shooting would start. Four fifty-nine.

He lowered the visor on his helmet, and gripped the gun firmly. His hands were dry. He moved forward slowly, hugging the curb, his left hand tight on the handlebar. The poodle appeared, followed by Zucca. He felt suddenly cold inside. Zucca saw him coming. He stopped at the edge of the sidewalk, holding back the dog. By the time he realized, it was too late. His mouth formed a circle, but no sound emerged. His eyes widened with fear. If he'd crapped in his pants, that would have been enough. He pressed the trigger. Disgusted with himself, with Zucca, with all men, all mankind. He emptied the clip into the guy's chest.

In front of the villa, the Mercedes shot forward. To his right, the bus was coming. It passed the stop, without slowing down. He accelerated, cut across the path of the bus, and went around it. He almost had to mount the sidewalk, but he got through. The bus came to an abrupt halt, stopping the Mercedes from entering the street. He rode flat out, turning left, then left again, onto Chemin du Souvenir, then Rue des Roses. On Rue des Bois-Sacrés, he threw the gun into a manhole. A few minutes later, he was riding calmly along Rue d'Endoume.

It was only then that he started thinking about Lole. You stood facing each other. You'd both gone beyond words. You wanted her belly against yours. You wanted the taste of her body. The smell. Mint and basil. But there were too many years between you, and too much silence. And Manu. Dead, yet still so alive. You were standing two feet apart. You could have put out your hand and taken her by the waist and drawn her to you. She could have untied the belt of her bathrobe and dazzled you with the beauty of her body. You'd have made love, violently, with unassuaged desire. But what would have happened afterwards? You'd have had to find words. Words that didn't exist. You'd have lost her forever. So you left. Without saying goodbye. Without a kiss. For the second time.

He was shaking. He pulled up outside the first bistro he came to on Boulevard de La Corderie. Like an automaton, he locked the moped and took off his helmet. He had a cognac. He felt the burning sensation spread through him. The cold flowed out of his body. He began to sweat. He rushed to the toilets and threw up. Threw up all he'd done, all he'd thought. Threw up the man that he was. The man who'd abandoned Manu and hadn't had the courage to love Lole. He'd drifted for so long. Too long. He knew that the worst was yet to come. By the second cognac, he'd stopped shaking. He'd recovered.

He parked at Fontaine-de-Caylus. It was 6:20, but the Arab kids weren't there, which surprised him. He took off his helmet and hooked it on the handlebars, but didn't cut the engine. The youngest of the Arabs appeared, kicking a ball. He ran up to him.

"Get out of here, the pigs are coming. They've been watching your girlfriend's house."

He set off, back up the alley. They must be watching all the back streets. Montée des Accoules, Traverse des Repenties. Place de Lenche, of course. He'd forgotten to ask Lole if Frankie Malabe had come back. He might have a chance if he took Rue des Cartiers, right up at the top. He left the moped and ran down the steps. There were two of them, two young plainclothes cops, at the bottom of the steps.

"Police!"

He heard the siren, higher up the street. He was trapped. Car doors slammed. They were here. Behind his back.

"Don't move!"

He did what he had to do. He plunged his hand inside his jacket. He had to get it over with. No more running. He was here. He was home. In his own neighborhood. It might as well be here. Might as well end in Marseilles. He turned toward the two young cops. The ones behind him couldn't see that he was unarmed. The first bullet ripped open his back. His lung exploded. He didn't feel the other two bullets.

From *At the End of a Dull Day*

By Massimo Carlotto

Translated from the Italian
by Antony Shugaar

Ruby Heartstealer taught us one more time:
Screwing the powerful is never a crime
(graffiti in blue paint on a wall in Padua)

At the end of a dull day, the lawyer and, incidentally, parliamentarian of the Italian republic Sante Brianese strode briskly into La Nena. A moment later his secretary and his personal assistant both appeared in the doorway. Ylenia and Nicola. Good-looking, well dressed, young, and cheerful. They looked like something straight out of an American TV show.

It was aperitif time in the establishment, and there was a steady flow of customers, drinks, and hors d'oeuvres. Outside on the patio, mushroom-shaped heat lamps kept the large crowd of smokers warm. I knew almost everybody there. I'd cultivated my clientele over the years with painstaking diligence. In my bar you'd never find cocaine, whores, or dickheads, and I had a bodybuilder on salary who might have fried his brains out on steroids but who still could be relied upon to stand discreetly outside the door and keep away vendors peddling flowers, cigarette lighters, and bric-a-brac of all kinds. You could only get into La Nena if you were looking to pay reasonable prices in exchange for a peaceful, refined, and yet "bubbly and amusing" atmosphere. Mornings, from 8 to 10, we served fine teas, fragrant croissants, and cappuccinos made with milk shipped directly to us from a small mountain village in the Dolomites. At noon sharp, the aperitif hour began. From 12:30 to 3 o'clock, we served lunch: a light, high-energy meal for office-workers and busy professionals, a minimalist vegetarian repast for fatties on perennial diets, or else a lavish banquet, in the strictest Venetian tradition, for salesmen and clients not worried about their weight. The evening aperitif began at 6:45 and dinner was served from 7:30 on. For ordinary mortals, the kitchen shut down at 10:30. For people like Brianese the restaurant was always open.

The Counselor took a seat at his usual table and his favorite waitress hurried over with the usual glass of fine prosecco that I'd been serving him free of charge for the past eleven years. Then, as usual, the customers lined up to pay their customary respects to their elected representative. Not all of the customers. There was a time when the ritual would have included every single customer in my establishment, but in the upcoming regional elections his party was facing a serious challenge from the Padanos, as they were affectionately dubbed even by their allies. More than a few of my clients were discreetly announcing their shift in allegiance to new masters. Brianese, with the usual smile stamped on his face, accepted the avowals of loyalty and kept a mental checklist of the defectors. Toward the end, it was my turn. I poured myself a glass of prosecco, walked around from behind the bar, and took a seat by his side.

"Things still tough down in Rome?" I asked.

He shrugged. "No worse than usual. The real challenges are up here now," he replied, watching his aides mix with the crowd. With a toolkit of wisecracks and gossip they were doing their best to herd the stragglers back into the fold. They knew their job and they were good at it, but victory was by no means assured. Only on election day would it be possible to reckon the exact percentage of the defeat and the collateral damage in terms of business. Then he turned to look me right in the eye and said: "We need to talk."

"Name a time, Counselor."

"Not now, I'm expecting guests. There'll be four of us, and we'll need the back room."

It was the most exclusive part of La Nena, entirely at the service of Brianese and the business consortiums and cabals that he controlled. I jutted my chin in Ylenia and Nicola's direction. Brianese shook his head. "No, they'll be going home. I have an appointment with three developers."

"Should I tell Nicoletta to come?"

"I feel sure that the gentlemen would appreciate the gesture."

I circled back behind the bar and pulled open a drawer. In it was the cell phone that I use only when I'm calling her.

Nicoletta Rizzardi was an old friend. She was one of the first people I met when I first moved to the Veneto. We'd even been lovers, for a short while. A tall, slender drink of water with a nice big pair of milky white boobs. She'd been divorced for years and was a die-hard smoker. She loved flashy expensive scarves which she wore constantly and with considerable flair. She had worked in the sector of high-end fashion—strictly counterfeits. Then came the wave of competition in that field from African immigrant street vendors, selling the same articles as she was but at half the price. She was forced to move into a new field and settle for a position repping mid-market intimate apparel. Her income dropped accordingly and she'd been scraping by until I approached her with a proposal to go into business with me in a certain endeavor that quickly proved to be a brilliant opportunity and a steady source of income for both of us.

One night when I was talking with Brianese I'd had the brainstorm. The Counselor was complaining about the fact that in this country public figures no longer enjoyed freedom or any right to privacy. Gossip had become the Italian national sport and no politician could afford the risk anymore of having a little fun on the side because of the danger of winding up as fodder for the press. An innocent dalliance could easily turn into the epitaph of a career. Maybe not in Lombardy or Rome, where members of parliament caught dabbling in extramarital sex or snorting lines of cocaine were exonerated by their fellow politicos as "victims of the pressure cooker life they led, unwillingly separated from their families." Here in the Veneto, however, there was just one simple rule: "do whatever you want, but don't get caught or it's curtains." The real problem came with the call girls themselves. They had become an integral part of the way business was conducted but they constantly proved to be deeply unreliable. These days no one dreamed of obtaining a contract of any size, even for a miserable traffic circle, without kicking in a percentage in kind. Corruption had evolved and those who were willing to settle for cash payments were considered two-bit operators. Now even wives and offspring were eager to grab a little something for themselves when possible: new wallpaper for the house or a Japanese sports car. Everybody seemed to want an extra piece of baksheesh, a gift to console themselves over the fact that they'd become corrupt. But the call girls had become ground zero for investigating magistrates and investigative journalists, and they were such birdbrains that they seemed incapable of keeping their mouths shut. No matter how bad things got, the call girls were always willing to appear on a talk show to make matters worse.

Brianese was right, several times over. I'd worked for a while in a lap dance club and I know a thing or two about the mindset you find in girls who are willing to accept that transaction.

So I took advantage of my experience and put together a small but extremely reliable network of prostitutes under the guise of an escort service. I went to work for Brianese and his friends.

Never more than four girls at a time, exclusively foreigners who knew nobody and were completely ignorant about the city, and we replaced them after exactly six months. Venezuelans, Argentines, and Brazilians with European features, preferably of Italian descent, the offspring of emigrants. And always one Chinese girl for that exotic touch.

The hard part about the Chinese girl was finding one who was even halfway presentable. I had a contact in Prato but he had nothing to show me but girls they were sending to work out of apartments. The problem was this: the Chinese girls assigned as sex workers were just the ones who couldn't keep up with production in the sweatshops, the ones who could no longer earn their keep. In other words, all I had to choose from was an array of twenty-two-year-old girls with chapped, callused hands who were so beaten down it would have taken a couple of months of rest and relaxation to get them into any kind of shape to spread their legs with at least a hint of a smile on their lips. I always found myself struggling to imagine them nicely made-up, their hair done properly by a professional hairdresser, and decently dressed. In other words, it was a thankless task, but these days you couldn't hope to operate a first-class escort service without at least one Chinese girl. They helped to put the most demanding clients at their ease and they were perfect for clients who had a hard time expressing their desires. Nicoletta described the Chinese girls as "the dolls that Italian males grew up wishing they could play with." That was true only in part. Actually, they were just sex slaves with long practice at satisfying their master's wishes. Now, my South American girls I got from Mikhail, a Russian in his forties who was as big, strong, and cunning as the Devil himself. Mikhail worked as a gofer and fixer for a prostitution ring run by two former hookers from Naples, in cahoots with one of the most powerful cops in town, who offered them protection. Mikhail let me pick my girls out of a catalogue and, when he was planning the international arrivals, he would just add mine to the list and keep the money for himself. Mikhail warned me against Russian prostitutes. He could of course get me all the Russian girls I wanted. In his homeland prostitution was a thriving institution, completely out of control. Leaving professional prostitutes aside, there was an army of Russian women of all ages willing to trade sexual favors for minor privileges, especially in the workplace. But once they were incorporated into my network, they'd start looking around for clients of their own and become rivals or else they'd find a man willing to keep them.

"Stick to South American girls," he'd told me. "They're less work. As I'm sure you know, the most important thing about whores is to pick them carefully because they can be a tremendous pain in the ass."

I liked the Russian guy; he was cautious and fair-minded. We regularly met in a large highway service plaza not far outside of Bologna. Lots of people coming and going at all hours. I'd park in an area that wasn't monitored by closed-circuit cameras, he'd slip into the car with his laptop under his arm, and he'd start an extended monologue about his name. I'd always assumed it wasn't his real name.

He claimed his full name was Mikhail Aleksandrovich Sholokhov, just like the Russian author who won the Nobel Prize for Literature in 1965.

"Why would the Swedes give the prize to a Communist?" he'd ask me each time with exaggerated indignation. "I can understand a dissident, but what's the idea of giving the award to a man who was named a Hero of the Soviet Union not once but twice?"

"No one even remembers his name," I replied.

"It's a good thing. I'd be embarrassed if anyone ever noticed that I have the same name as that guy. You know that I went into a bookshop once and asked for his best-known book, *And Quiet Flows the Don*?"

"It must be out of print," I said, starting to sound like a broken record.

"Which is lucky, too. Do you think they'll reprint it?"

"No way. Who cares about a writer from the Soviet era? Now Putin's in charge, and he happens to be a close friend of our current prime minister."

"Yeah, and your prime minister ought to learn a lesson from Putin about the best way to eliminate the danger of scandals," he shot back. "'Eliminate' . . . I don't know if you catch the pun . . ."

He laughed long and loud. At last, he turned on his laptop so he could show me the catalogue.

"All right, now let's talk about women and money, the only two good things about our lives."

I always played along. I knew Mikhail put on that routine so he'd have time to see if there were any detectives lurking in the shadows.

On his laptop, there were nude photographs of each girl in six different poses, so that their best and worst features were clearly evident. The ones who came to work for us were lucky. We sent them to live in comfortable spacious homes, where Nicoletta took personal charge of them. She taught them everything they needed to know about clothing, make-up, perfume, and etiquette. When they weren't busy with paying clients, Nicoletta gave them work modeling her line of intimate apparel, which served as excellent cover. It was also a good way to make them feel special and to ward off the boredom that could quickly turn into depression. Depression could fill their heads with ideas that were bad for business. To date, in fact, none of the girls had caused trouble and it had never been necessary to use my fists on any of them. When my partner and I welcomed each new group we made sure that they couldn't miss a shiny pair of brass knuckles apparently left out in plain view on a coffee table—by accident. Even rank beginners knew that brass knuckles were a whore's worst enemy.

Our girls weren't cheap. Whether it was for five minutes or the whole night, the price never changed: two hundred fifty euros; out of that fee, two hundred euros, no less, went directly into the girl's pockets. Despite the high price, none of our customers had ever complained. They were happy to pay extra for a guarantee of discretion. Anyway the money never came out of the customer's wallet. It was always part of the cost of doing business.

The security rules were iron bound. No drugs, just champagne. Cell phones to be left in the car so that some imbecile couldn't take pictures or compromising videos. The encounters took place in various detached villas, scattered throughout the various provinces and rented for short periods through a real estate agency where Nicoletta's brother worked. Only rarely in hotels. When the girls weren't busy entertaining politicians and friends of politicians, they were made available to prosperous foreign industrialists. The company rule was this: only one client a day, but seven days a week.

The girls fooled themselves into believing they'd become princesses until the morning I loaded them into my car, pretending I was taking them to an orgy outside of town and, once I got them to Genoa, selling them to a group of Maltese gangsters for twice what I'd paid for them. I never asked what would happen to them. All I knew was that a few hours later they were already on board a freighter heading for the Maghreb region of northwest Africa or to Spain. That was all that mattered to me.

The minute the girls got out of the car and found themselves surrounded by those ugly mugs in the filthy warehouse that served as the gang's headquarters, they immediately understood the cruel trap they'd been lured into and they began to weep and wail. It was a heartbreaking spectacle, but it only amused the buyers. They laughed heartily as they reached out rough, dirty hands to grab and grope, savoring the impending rape. For that matter, they were old-school gangsters, firmly convinced that if a whore got a taste of hell, then she'd mistake the clients for heavenly angels. At that juncture, I'd point that they were taking delivery of delicate, valuable merchandise, count my money in a hurry, and hop in my car and head home.

Every time, the Maltese gangsters asked me to point out the finest of the group, the one that they assumed had spent the most time in my bed. I'd point to one at random, because the last thing I would dream of doing was fuck any of them. After all, I was the boss, and picking one in particular would have just created bad group dynamics. I didn't want any of them getting it into her head that she was my favorite. But because when all was said and done I was the boss, even though we were theoretically equal partners, every month, after splitting the take, I demanded that Nicoletta give me a first-class blowjob. It was a good way of reminding her whose idea it had been. After all, it was a profitable little operation. At year's end, after expenses, I pocketed about a hundred thousand euros, but I was forced to plow about half of that sum back into the restaurant. La Nena had turned into a money pit. The economic downturn was having its effect, even though the Veneto was doing better than many other parts of the country. It was damned expensive to keep up certain standards of quality. My biggest expense was staff. To say nothing of the wine cellar. It wasn't like the good old days. Now even people who could afford the finest still avoided the more expensive bottles. Only when bribers and bribees were drinking to the success of a negotiation was price truly no object. Even then, they demanded only the best. Especially the ones who had never been able to get a seat at the main table to shovel forkfuls of the angelfood cake of corruption into their gaping maws: they always seemed to know all about the latest fashions in wine. I made sure I always had plenty of the latest thing in stock.

Nothing on earth that could have convinced me to give up La Nena. It was solid proof that my life had changed for good, a calling card that gave me a respected status in society. In the year 2000, thanks to Brianese and his hefty fee, I obtained legal rehabilitation. My personal history as a former terrorist sentenced to life imprisonment without parole was expunged from my record. At the end of a long and twisted series of events, during which I'd worked like a mule, I had become an upright citizen and the proprietor of a fashionable establishment in the heart of a city in the Venetian provinces. I voted in elections and I paid my taxes. And with a series of smiles, ass-lickings, and lots of hard work, I won acceptance. I was now "one of them." And not just any one of them. I was a winner. One of the people you couldn't pretend you hadn't seen or forget to say hello to.

Nicoletta picked up on the third ring. With her voice made hoarse from too many cigarettes, she always sounded as if she'd just gotten out of bed.

"How many and where?" she asked.

"All four, and tonight they don't have to travel."

"Understood. I'll get them ready."

I went to take their orders. Brianese had already put his guests at their ease and was explaining how he could intervene to help them win a number of contracts for school and army barracks renovations in a neighboring province. When I returned with the wine, they'd already struck a deal for a 3 percent cut and now they were talking about the right gifts to give each official. The building commissioner had made it known that he expected a year's worth of landscaping services.

Waiting for me at the bar was my wife, Martina, fiddling with her aperitif glass. I gave her a smile and a kiss on the lips—lips that tasted of Campari.

"Ciao, darling."

Then I said hello to Gemma, the friend who had come in

with her, and pointed to a table where a well dressed, austere-looking gentleman was dining alone. "Do you mind eating with Professor Salvini? He's the new chief pediatrician, he's just moved to town, and he doesn't know anybody."

The doctor was glad to welcome them to his table. Knowing Gemma, I assumed that within five minutes she'd know all about the physician's personal life. She'd been on the prowl for a stable relationship ever since her husband dumped her and moved south to the Salento district of Puglia, where he now lived with his new girlfriend. Luckily, Martina could step in and keep Gemma from taking things too far. Martina and I had been married for nine years and she came in every day to eat lunch and dinner at my place. The kitchen in our apartment was used only for breakfast in the morning and for an infrequent herbal tea at night. If it was up to her, Martina would have been thrilled to cook meals and host lunches and dinners for friends and relatives, but I always opposed the idea vehemently. I didn't see the point of getting a bunch of pots and pans dirty when there was an excellent restaurant available. The waitress came over to ask what my wife would be having this evening. I always ordered for her. I did my best to take care of every aspect of her life. It was my way of showing her how much I loved her. And how grateful I was to her. She'd been there for me at one of the most difficult points in my life, when Roberta, the woman I was about to marry, died suddenly. A tragic accident snatched her away from me. She had an aspirin allergy, and she'd accidentally ingested a fatal overdose at my house. Because of my past, and due to unfounded suspicions on the part of her parents and the parish priest, whom Roberta considered her spiritual guide, I was investigated for murder and persecuted by two overzealous non-commissioned Carabinieri officers. I was lucky that Counselor Brianese stepped in and settled the case. My fiancée had actually introduced me to Martina. At the time, Martina was dating a guy with a poncey accent. Even though we were both involved with other people, something clicked between us and we had a meaningless little fling. It may have been meaningless but it did give me a useful piece of information: unlike my bride-to-be Roberta, Martina was passionate in bed. I saw her again at the funeral; she was at my side the whole time, consoling me and holding my hand.

A few months later, by the time my grief over Roberta's death had faded into a giant blank, we started dating and one night I asked her to marry me.

Actually, I was just planning to live with her, but Brianese had insisted on a proper marriage. That way, people would be more likely to forget about my past and about Roberta. I entrusted the logistics and details of the happiest day of our lives to Nicoletta and everything went off without a hitch. Refined, a little dull for most of the guests, and exhausting for the newlyweds. My lawyer was my best man and Gemma was Martina's maid of honor.

When we got back from our honeymoon in Polynesia we moved to the new house, not far from La Nena and, as we had solemnly vowed, we started taking care of one another.

The first thing I did was advise Martina to quit her job. Her monthly salary of 1,500 euros wouldn't change a thing in our lives and it would only come between us. She didn't want to stop working at first but in the end I convinced her that it was the best thing to do. She was especially worried that she'd be bored.

"That'll never happen, my love."

Just like any other couple, getting to know one another and accepting the shortcomings of your spouse was a challenge, but we were in love and in the end we overcame every hurdle. One of the biggest challenges was Gemma and I'd been forced to play my cards with great cunning to curb her negative influence over my wife. Martina had always told me every last detail about her best friend and I knew that things weren't going well in her marriage in that period. So, with admirable generosity, I'd helped her to find a new apartment, a job, and a good lawyer. When Gemma came to thank me I made it clear to her that the time had come for her to be a friend to both of us. I needed an ally to help me maintain a balance in our happy married life.

"I don't like what I'm hearing," she said. "I've been close to Martina since middle school. She's my best friend, and you're just an acquaintance to me . . ."

I raised one hand to stop her. "If I tell her to stop seeing you for good, she'll do as I say. And right now you don't have any other best friends, or even a man, for that matter."

"Martina doesn't have any other close friends either," she shot back in annoyance.

"But I can buy her all the friends I want and I can deprive you of everything you have."

Gemma turned pale and bit her lip to keep from crying, but I hastened to add: "I'm not looking for a fight. But you know that Martina has a complicated personality and she needs time to wrap her mind around certain concepts."

"So you want me to help convince her that you're always right."

"Gemma, I *am* always right. I work all day, year round, and I need someone to go on vacation with her . . . Winters, summers, weekends . . . all expenses paid, of course."

"I wish I could just tell you to go fuck yourself," she said under her breath.

I gave her an affectionate pat on the cheek. "But you won't do that because I'm making your life easier and more comfortable. Look at yourself: you smoke too much, you're overweight, you always drink at least one spritz too many, you're obviously unhappy, and without Martina and her adorable husband, you'll only go downhill."

At that point, true to the script, she tried to justify herself, find a reason to be able to look herself in the face in the bathroom mirror every morning. "But you do love her at least?"

"I'm crazy about her. Why do you think I'd ever behave in such an odious fashion? Because I can't afford to lose her."

And for once I'd told the truth, even if it was just a line from an old movie. Living with Martina, taking care of her had brought a little peace into my life, but most important it had laid to rest those impulses I'd been unable to control in the past and that still surfaced now and then, even though I no longer needed to get drunk on violence and cruelty in order to feel I was alive.

FROM *MINOTAUR*

By Benjamin Tammuz

Translated from the Hebrew
by Kim Parfitt and Mildred Budny

A MAN, WHO was a secret agent, parked his hired car in a rain-drenched square and took a bus into town. That day he had turned forty-one, and as he dropped into the first seat he came across, he closed his eyes and fell into bleak contemplation of his birthday. The bus pulled up at the next stop, jerking him back to consciousness, and he watched as two girls sat down on the empty seat in front of him. The girl on the left had hair the color of copper—dark copper with a glint of gold. It was sleek and gathered at the nape of her neck with a black velvet ribbon, tied in a cross-shaped bow. This ribbon, like her hair, radiated a crisp freshness, a pristine freshness to be found in things as yet untouched by a fingering hand. Whoever tied that ribbon with such meticulous care? wondered the man of forty-one. Then he waited for the moment when she would turn her profile to her friend, and when she turned to her friend and he saw her features, his mouth fell open in a stifled cry. Or did it perhaps escape from his mouth? Anyway, the passengers did not react.

2.

Today I'm forty-one and this is not the first time I've celebrated my birthday filling in a diary in a hotel room. Tomorrow I'll find a greetings telegram at the embassy from my wife and the two girls. And there'll be a special telegram from my son at boarding school. He is also away from home, and if he likes it that way, no doubt he'll follow in my footsteps. If he does, there'll be another reason for me to end it all as soon as possible. Except that early this evening it finally happened, and now I want to hang on.

I don't know why I believed that before meeting her I would receive some sort of advance notice. At any rate, it never occurred to me that I might be taken by surprise. But I was. I saw her quite suddenly, sitting down in front of me on the bus. I had no difficulty whatsoever in recognizing her. When she got off the bus I followed her. I have already found out her address and tomorrow I shall also know her surname and possibly even her Christian name. She lives in a smart building, the kind where the well-off live. I heard her speaking to her friend and even her voice gave her away. She might well sing in a choir. Her accent bears witness to a good education; her clothes are simple but expensive. Not a single ornament, apart from a black velvet ribbon: a somber ribbon tied with a marvelous precision that gave the desired impression—carelessness. The color of her hair is just as I remembered it, and so is the color of her eyes—a deep brown, not too dark. Her chin juts out a little, just far enough to leave no doubts about the kind of person she is: of sufficient character to dismiss anything unwanted but, above all, capable of wholehearted and passionate devotion. Her coloring and complexion are as I remembered them: very fair, like my mother's, with a pink bloom deepening, flawless and unhurried, toward high cheekbones, so gradually that it is impossible to say where white turns to pink. But her mouth is a sudden, vivid crimson. And those teeth. My God! Surely they cannot have been created just to chew food. If they were, I'd say that there was no need to go to so much trouble.

And I am forty-one and she is about seventeen. Twenty-four years.

3.

Thea,

This letter, which is typewritten, is not signed and I daresay we shall never meet. Yet I have seen you and I made sure that you saw me. That was about six weeks ago. I walked past you and you looked at me, the way you look at people coming toward you in the street. You didn't recognize me. But even so, you belong to me.

You will never have an opportunity to ask me questions, but my voice will reach you through my letters, and I know that you will read them. How do I know? I can offer no explanation, other than what I am about to tell you: for as long as I can remember I have been searching for you. I knew you existed, but I didn't know where. My work brought me to the town where you live. My work is a series of surmises, assumptions, and risks. I chose this work because I have never loved anyone, except you, although all my life I have been trying to love—in other words, to be unfaithful to you. I have devoted my life to tough and disagreeable work because I needed to love. And therefore I love the country I serve, her mountains, her valleys, her dust and despair, her roads and her paths. I acted as I did through lack of choice. I didn't know if I would ever meet you. And now, now that we have met, it's too late. There has been a mistake, some sort of discrepancy in birth dates, in passports. Even heaven is chaotic, just like any other office. Anyway, it's too late and it's quite impossible.

I have the address of your boarding school and I also know which university you will be attending next year. And I know that you like music. In due course I shall know still more.

With this letter there will be a parcel, containing a record player and a record. I'd like you to play the record next Sunday at 1700 hours. I shall do the same in my hotel room, not far from you, and the two of us will be listening to the same music at the very same time. This will be our first meeting, and I shall know if you have done as I asked. Indeed, I already know that you will respond to this appeal.

I love you. I have loved you all my life. It is difficult for me to come to terms with the thought that you did not recognize me in the street. But that's not your fault. There has been a mistake: in dates, in places, in everything. I'm quite sure that it was me who was intended to be tormented, not you.

I take your shoe off your foot and kiss your toes. I know them, just as I know every line of your body. Don't be angry, don't take pity. I never knew happiness until I found you.

4.

Funny Man!

I did as you asked at 1700 hours precisely. How did you know that I am playing this concerto right now? For that matter, how do you come to know so much about everything? I've been trying to guess who you are and I think that I have it. If I am right you'll have to give in and come out into the open. You are G.R., and we met at a party at N.'s. I'm right, aren't I? You were looking at me all the time and they told me your name.

I don't have anywhere to send this letter, but I'm writing it so that I can show it to you if we ever meet. I'm writing because it's impolite not to answer a letter as nice as yours. (By the way, I hardly understood a word of it. You're awfully mysterious.) Meanwhile I'm putting my reply in a special box, marked "Letters to Mr. Anonymous," until we meet. It's not nice to keep a girl in suspense like this.

Yours,

Thea

5.

My anonymous friend,

I think you should know that I have exams soon and I can't answer every single one of your letters, especially when you write every day, sometimes twice a day. I'm writing a general answer to all the letters that have come so far and, until the exams are over, I shan't write anymore, and you will just have to forgive me.

Now I am sure that you are not G.R., because in the meantime he has introduced himself to me and performed all sorts of amorous maneuvers. And so you remain unidentified and I am angry because your letters are becoming so sad and I'd like to tell you that there is no need to take me so seriously. Lately I've been looking in the mirror a lot, to find out what you see in me, and do you know what I discovered? I should be ashamed of myself, but it's true. I discovered that maybe I really am prettier than I thought. And this is all your fault. Now it's difficult for me to enjoy the compliments I get from my friends because, compared to your letters, everything they say sounds crude. Although I don't know you, I am sure that you are cleverer than all my friends, but I sometimes think that you exaggerate terribly. And why are you so sad? If you wanted, you could be a writer or a poet, even if you don't mean what you write.

And why do you talk about wanting to die? If you love me, as you say in all your letters, you simply have to show your face. Perhaps I'll like you? Why all this bizarre mystery? You seem to explain everything, but I understand nothing. I'm not as bright as you think.

And thanks so much for the other two records you sent. You seem to be crazy about this one composer, as you're always sending me his music. I agree that he is wonderful, and I play the records on Sundays at 1700 hours. All according to your madness. As you can see, I'm behaving like a good girl and it's about time that you were a good boy too and sent me a photo at least.

Your friend,
Thea

P.S. This letter is going into the "Letters to Mr. Anonymous" box too. How much longer will you be anonymous?

6.

Dearest Mr. Anonymous,

I have finished my exams and now I shall sit about listening to the records that have been piling up. Did you know that you are very impolite? This is the third letter I have written to you in the past year and I still have no address to send them to.

I know no more about you today than I did after receiving your first letter. But there is a big difference: If you were to stop writing to me now, I should miss you. Perhaps that's your intention? You make me feel like a queen and I'm getting used to it. Where will it all end? No one but you knows all the fine qualities you see in me. You are making me grow accustomed to something no one else will ever give me. Why are you doing it? I shan't write to you anymore unless you come and introduce yourself. This is the last letter I'm putting in the "Letters to Mr. Anonymous" box. Now I'm going to play a record and I hope that you will be playing one at the same time. Then you'll understand that I want to see you, without any obligation, of course. In spite of everything you're still a dear.

Your friend,
Thea

7.

Thea,

I must beg your forgiveness for the contents of the last two letters. I had no right to involve you in my weeping and wailing. I am ashamed of myself and promise never to do such a thing again.

I dreamed about you last night. I was standing alone on a balcony and you appeared in the doorway, looked at me, and smiled. Then you came toward me. You didn't really walk but float through the air till you reached my side. You didn't embrace me or reach out to me but lean slightly toward me and kiss me on the lips; I burst into tears, and you smiled and said, "I belong to you. Take me." I said, "How can I take you?" And you said, "In the air. Take me in the air."

What did you mean, Thea? Two weeks ago I saw the graduation ceremony at your school. I was sitting in the third row, on the right, not far from your parents. When you looked at them your eyes rested momentarily on my face. Thank you, my love. I kissed you in the air, just as you suggested in my dream. You didn't recognize me. Once again you didn't recognize me.

I shall be in town in a few months' time. I shall not go to your university, because there it would be easy to pick out a stranger. On that wretched campus you will be lost to me for a long time. I'll try to see you during vacations when you come home for holidays. I know you will not be angry about all this absurd mystery that surrounds me. It's not a mystery at all. There is simply no other way. There is not, believe me.

I love you.

8.

Thea,

It is three years today since I found you. You are my greatest loss, a loss that was recovered only when it was already too late. Only today did it occur to me that you might perhaps like to write to me once. So this is what I suggest you do: write on the envelope "Mr. Franz Kafka, Poste Restante," and send it to your local post office. I shall be there on December 5th. At 1700 hours I shall go to the post office to collect your letter. In order to be sure that you don't come to identify me, I would like you to sit in the café opposite your parents' home at that time. One of my friends will go there to confirm that you are doing as I ask. He will phone me and then I shall go to the post office and collect your letter. If you are not in the café, I shall not go to the post office. Forgive me if my suspicions are groundless.

9.

Thea,

The girl you sent to the post office to identify me did not see me but one of my friends. In the post office we saw a girl keeping a lookout and I realized that you were trying to outwit me. You have no idea how grateful I am for the fact that you wanted to see me and that you went to so much trouble. Even in my misfortune I am the happiest man in the world.

I have read your letters. You are as kind as I expected, you are as lovely as I know you to be, you are not my mistake, Thea. In my work I must never misjudge people's characters, because if I were to make a mistake even once, I might have to pay for it with my life. If I had been wrong about you I should have been dead a long time ago.

I want to answer all your questions but I cannot answer them in the way that you suggest. What I do have to say is this: I know that besides the things that we can readily understand, examine, analyze, and make use of, there is within us—and perhaps also outside us—a conscious force infinitely wiser than the intellect at our disposal. I collaborate with this force every day, especially in my work. And if I am still alive, it means that this force is not an illusion. It is likely to bring about my downfall, I suppose, but it's the best guide I have, the one that has shown you to me for as long as I remember. And it is a fact that you really do exist, exactly as I knew you before I found you. I need no better proof than this.

At the same time something has gone wrong, a mistake or a deliberate punishment. At any rate, we can't be what we were meant to be. We can't meet and we can't be united. The reason for this is simple, mundane, and humiliating, but I don't want to spell it out, because if I do, you will know that I am afraid and then you will doubt my love. There, I have already said too much.

I love you, Thea. If there is a God, he will make us meet in the place where I first divined or dreamed of you, before you were even born. If he will not make this gesture on our behalf, it means that he is not God, or that he does not exist, or that he is nothing but an office—efficient but indifferent.

You exist and every day I kiss your fingers and your toes. Soon I shall dare to touch your cheeks. I shall do it first with my hand and then with my lips. I hope to dream of you tonight.

10.

About four years after the secret agent met Thea, G.R. asked her to marry him. Her parents gave their consent and the wedding was arranged for the beginning of winter.

About a month before the wedding G.R. was killed in a car

crash. The same week Thea submitted her final dissertation to the university. Shortly after the death of her fiancé she went to Gstadt with her parents, and when they reached the hotel, she found a bouquet of roses waiting for her and a box of chocolates with a letter.

Thea,

God wants you to be happy so you must get over this. You will find peace of mind in your walks around the district. You are young and intelligent. There can be no doubt that you will get over it.

I have no right to bother you with words now, and I certainly have no right to set you any unnecessary riddles, and so I shall say only this, in order to put your mind at rest. You will be wondering about the bouquet that was waiting for you at the hotel. Well, it's quite simple. I learn about your actions, your movements, and your plans from various people around you. I pay them for their trouble. And to make things even simpler, I shall give you an example. In the café opposite your house there used to be an old waiter. He has since died, so I am not afraid to reveal his identity. He used to receive regular payments in exchange for the reports he gave me on whatever he managed to find out. People like that are to be found everywhere and people like myself do not hesitate to make use of their services.

Don't be angry, it's the only way open to me. I travel a lot and I'm not a permanent resident in your country. If I had relied on chance alone, I would have lost you long ago. I am satisfied with what chance gave me when I found you.

Please smile, my angel. Smile, even in your grief, at me, at yourself, and at all that's terrible and wonderful in this our destiny.

P.S. Next Sunday I shall be in the district. If you need anything or if you want to write to me, leave your letter at the post office and at 1700 hours I shall go and collect it. You are to sit in the café below the hotel. Our usual arrangement.

11.

My anonymous friend, my only friend at this time,

Thank you for the flowers and the chocolates. I told my parents that they were from university friends. There, because of you I lied to them, and not for the first time. No one in the world would ever understand what there is between us. I don't really understand it myself, but do I have any choice?

The tragic death of G.R. was seven times worse because I saw it as divine retribution. I don't understand why G.R. was punished and not I, because I had sinned against him and not he against me. I was about to marry him without being really in love with him. I was very fond of him as I told you in my letters but my love for him was not deep enough to justify marriage. This God that you call an office, for some reason, probably got the wrong address. Why did poor G.R. have to give his life to prevent the wrong I was about to do him? My anonymous friend, I am not as wonderful as you make me out to be. Now you see that I am small and pitiable and even ugly. What do I have to smile about? I wrote my final dissertation on Luis de Góngora, as you know, and when I saw G.R. pale and dead I thought,

Un cuerpo con poca sangre
Pero con dos corazones,*

and at the same time I told myself quite shamelessly that it was not about G.R. that de Góngora wrote this marvelous verse.

*A body with little blood/But with two hearts.

If I thought that G.R. had had two hearts, I might have loved him with all of my one.

I'm writing this letter in the café where I shall be sitting on Sunday at 1700 hours and I am amusing myself with the thought that you might be here now, among the dozens of people in the room, or that you are outside looking in at me through the window. Look how you dominate me, my anonymous friend. You are cruel when all's said and done, and the worst of it is that I don't believe you and I still think that we shall meet in the end. If you disappoint me I shall never forgive you.

From *Carte Blanche*
By Carlo Lucarelli

Translated from the Italian
by Michael Reynolds

Chapter One

The bomb exploded with a ferocious blast right as the funeral procession was crossing the street. De Luca threw himself to the ground, instinctively, and covered his head with his hands as a section of wall collapsed onto the sidewalk, showering him in dust. Everybody started shouting. A sergeant from the Republican National Guard stretched a machine gun out over De Luca's body and fired an endless burst that deafened him and brought a deluge of broken pantiles down onto the street.

"Bastards," the sergeant cried. "Sons of bitches!"

"Bastardi!" everybody cried, all of them shooting: the GNR, the Black Brigades, the Decima Mas marines, the police. All of them except De Luca, on the ground with his face in the dust, his hands open on his head, his fingers stuck in his hair. He remained like that for an interminable moment, and only when everybody had stopped shooting and all that could be heard were the moans of the injured, only then did he lift himself to his knees, brushing the dust off his trench coat, and get back to his feet.

"They'll pay for this!" a striper cried into his face, grabbing him by the lapels of his coat. "Retaliation! Carte blanche!"

"Carte blanche, right," said De Luca, freeing himself from the hysterical grip that was stripping him of his clothes. "Sure, sure."

He moved away quickly, without turning back, sighing through lips that tasted of dust. His knee hurt. Knew I shouldn't have stopped to watch, he thought, and turned the corner as the first trucks stopped with a screech of brakes and the Germans leapt out to close off the streets.

De Luca threw his hands deep into his pockets and pulled his trench coat tight as spring was late arriving that year and it was still cold. He turned another corner and counted down the building numbers to fifteen. He mounted the first step, went back to check the number again—via Battisti, 15—then entered resolutely. He passed by an elevator with its cage and commanding wrought-iron gate and stopped in front of the porter's window, but there was nobody in. He started up a flight of stairs—white and exceptionally clean, like marble. A high-class building. And for contrast's sake, running his hand over his stubbly chin, he thought it was time to get himself a shave. On the first floor, a man came towards him; he was big, he wore a heavy overcoat and had a square policeman's face.

"What happened?" asked the man, alarmed. "That noise outside . . ."

"An attack," De Luca said. "They threw a bomb at Tornago's funeral. But everything's under control now."

"Ah, okay." The man shook his head, as if he were about to say something else, but then took a step forward and planted a hand against De Luca's chest as he made for the door, stopping him mid-stride with his leg out and a counterblow that hurt his neck.

"Hey there, friend! Where do you think you're going?"

De Luca closed his eyes, momentarily ironing out the creases that insomnia had etched on his face. He made a sign with his right hand as if to say "just a second," and with his left hand pulled a badge out of his pocket that the gorilla, turning white, recognized immediately, even before reading it. He stretched out his arm in salute, clicking his heels.

"Excuse me, Comandante. If you had told me at once . . ."

De Luca nodded and put away his badge.

"No harm done," he said, "but don't call me Comandante, I'm not with the Brigata Muti anymore. I'm with the police. This is my case. Who's inside?"

"Maresciallo Pugliese, from the Mobile Squad. And the team."

"No authorities? Journalists? Family?"

"Only the police."

"Good. Don't let anybody in . . . except me, that is. Let me through, please."

"Sorry. At your command, Comandante."

"Commissario, not Comandante. Commissario."

"Yes, sorry, sir. At your command, Commissario."

De Luca sighed as the gorilla moved to one side and opened the door. He entered a vestibule that was rather narrow, small, quite different to how he had imagined it. To one side of the entrance there was a white telephone sitting on a small, bow-legged side-table, on the other side a hat tree and several prints on the wall; at the far end, in a part of the room framed by the doorway, as if in a painting, there were two men. They watched De Luca as he approached. One was short with a bird's beak nose and a black hat, the other young, thin, wearing glasses.

"What happened?" asked the short one in a heavy southern accent. "A bomb?"

"An attack," De Luca repeated. "Grenades at Tornago's funeral."

"Only grenades?" said the thin fellow. "Sounded like the front had shifted here."

"They lost their heads and started shooting, all of them."

The thin one took off his glasses, shaking his head as he did so. "Someone'll have gotten killed, no doubt. They're in such bad shape that they're killing themselves. Even a funeral has become dangerous, even the funeral of an impor—" He stopped, because the short one, who was looking hard at De Luca with narrowed eyes, had squeezed his arm just above the elbow.

"Why, I know you, don't I?" he said, as De Luca got closer. "You're part of the Political Police. Is this your case, then? We're more than happy to hand it over to you. C'mon, Albertini, let's go."

De Luca held up his hand, stopping them at the doorstep with a deep sigh that was almost a groan.

"How many times must I repeat it today?" he said. "I'm not with the Political Police anymore, I'm Commissario De Luca, assigned to the police. They transferred me yesterday from the Brigata Ettore Muti, special division of the Political Police, and I don't have my papers yet, but we work together. They gave me this case. That okay?"

The beak-nosed man took his hat off, bowing his head. "At your command," he said. Albertini, on the other hand, didn't utter another word.

De Luca entered the room. There next to him, to his right, a man was lying face up on the floor against the wall, his arm bent upwards. He was dressed in a powder-blue silk dressing gown and he had a large, dark, sticky wound in his chest right over his heart. Another wound, in the groin, was partly visible under the bloodied flap of his dressing gown. De Luca looked at him at length, then let his gaze drift: the walls plastered with books, the writing desk with the glass lamp, the armchairs in the middle of the room, the coffee table, the chandelier, the mirrors, the rug, everything neat and tidy. It was a rich man's building, all right.

"Who is he?" De Luca asked, turning back to the corpse.

"Name's Rehinard," said the short man. Albertini had stopped talking altogether.

"German?"

"He was from Trento. Italian citizen."

"You know him?"

"No, I've got his wallet. Here."

From the entrance came a noise, but De Luca didn't turn.

"It's one of my men going through the other rooms," said the short man. "It's a big apartment, four rooms, the bathroom, the kitchen, and nobody in it but him. So, do you want this wallet?"

De Luca took the wallet of heavy, hand-tooled crocodile leather, and walked over to the coffee table in the middle of the room. He sat down in an armchair and emptied the wallet's contents onto the glass top beside two empty glasses. He noticed the rim of one was stained with lipstick.

"Papers," said the short man, as De Luca examined them. "Party membership card, money, and some visiting cards." One was most elegant, embossed in ornate lettering that read *Count Alberto Maria Tedesco*, and another more simple, smooth, with *Sibilla* written in italics and a telephone number. De Luca held the Count's card in his hand, as if weighing it, then dropped it down with the others.

"Where's the maid?"

"Excuse me?"

"The maid, the servant, the cleaning woman, what do you call her?"

The short man looked at De Luca strangely, frowning over his thin eyes. "There is no maid," he said.

"In a home this clean and tidy? A single man, a bachelor, according to the documents?" De Luca stood up and wandered around the room. "Seems too tidy to me for an hourly maid, unless she just left. Or maybe it's a manservant. One of the rooms may be his, his stuff'll be in it. Isn't there anything down at the station on this guy that you know of?"

"Not as far as I remember, and I remember everything. It's more likely that you have something on him. I mean . . ."

"As a matter of fact, there is, but not much." De Luca remembered the yellow record: Rehinard Vittorio, member of the PFR, the Fascist Republican Party, and that was it. He remembered it precisely for this reason. "The doctor been yet?" he asked.

"Not yet, but we've called him."

"And Maresciallo Pugliese?"

"That's me. Pugliese."

"Oh."

De Luca stopped again in front of the corpse. He looked at it, then moved aside the edge of the dressing gown covering his legs with the point of his shoe. Albertini turned away. Pugliese, instead, came closer, leaning forward, his hands on his knees.

"Jealousy?" he said. De Luca shrugged.

"Maybe," he mumbled. "A woman was here, and not long ago. I'd say a blond, judging from the color of the lipstick on that glass. There's no weapon, right?"

"No, we haven't found it yet, be it a stiletto or a knife."

"A paper knife."

"A paper knife?" Pugliese shot him another sidelong glance.

"Might very well be. It's the only thing missing from the writing desk, which really does have everything, and there are a couple of opened envelopes with today's date." De Luca went back to the coffee table and fell into an armchair. He drew his face to the lipstick-stained glass and gave it a keen sniff. Alcohol. At that hour of the morning? Strange. The other was empty. Suddenly, as had repeatedly been the case over the past week, a wave of sleep washed over him, making him yawn; always at the wrong time, never at night, when he would lie awake in bed watching the darkness on the ceiling, or tossing and turning, eyelids clamped shut, twisted up in his bed sheet.

"Who called you?" he asked.

"The porter," said Pugliese. "The one who discovered the body. He was passing by and saw the door wide open. He came in and saw everything. His wife telephoned us."

A balding man wearing lightweight spectacles came into the

room and stopped, looking first at De Luca and then at Pugliese, who returned his look with a nod.

"Nothing there," said the bald man. "Only the bathroom and one of the rooms look lived in, the others are empty."

"No other room? I don't know, women's stuff in the closet? Things like that?" De Luca asked, and Pugliese smiled when the bald man shook his head.

"Nothing. Only a bedroom with a man's belongings: clothes, toiletries, shoes . . ."

"Bed soiled?"

"Sorry?"

"Physiological marks on the sheets?"

"Oh, right. No, nothing. Everything in its place, even the bed is made."

"Hair in the brush?"

The bald man, annoyed, glanced at Pugliese. "Blond, straight, long, like on the head of the gentleman there."

De Luca nodded, collapsing back into the armchair. His head sank down between his shoulders, sagging down into the collar of his trench coat. He stretched his legs out, digging his heels into the floor, and he could have fallen asleep there and then, enveloped in a cloud of white, dusty fabric cut in two by his black shirt, his face wrinkled and unshaven slumping slowly towards his chest.

"Are you feeling all right?" said Pugliese. "You look rotten."

"Insomnia," murmured De Luca, "And not only that . . . but, don't worry, I'm not about to fall asleep. I was just thinking. We just have to talk to the porter and find out what kind of character this Rehinard was, who he saw and who was here this morning. And if he had a maid, because as far as I'm concerned something doesn't add up here."

Pugliese nodded vigorously. "Fine. And then?"

De Luca looked him straight in the eyes, serious. "And then, nothing. What more do you want to do? We have a rather well-off stiff on our hands, a party-member connected to Tedesco. You know Tedesco, right? Minister for Foreign Affairs . . . Look at how he's been killed: this promises to be a dirty case. Do you think an investigation is going to be possible? Or that anybody cares, at a moment like this, with the Americans almost to Bologna? I'll cut my own throat if they let us continue."

Pugliese smiled and opened his arms widely as De Luca put his hands on the armrests and in a sudden movement got to his feet, unsteadily.

"At your command," said Pugliese as he followed him to the door with his hat in hand. He stopped in front of the elevator, his finger nearly on the call button, but then hurried off on his short legs to catch up with De Luca, who was already halfway down the first flight of stairs.

"Comandante!" he wheezed. "Damn it! Sorry, Commissa, I can't seem to remember! Listen, Commissario, if you don't mind, when we're with the porter let me show him my badge. If they see yours, they'll scare and they won't talk at all."

De Luca didn't reply. They reached the porter's room and Pugliese rapped on the glass with his knuckles, but De Luca opened the door and went straight in, assailed by the stink of cooked cabbage and stale air that wrinkled his nose and turned his stomach. Inside, there was a gray-haired woman sitting on a wicker chair in front of a lighted stove with a rosary in her hand. She gave the impression of looking older than she was.

"Good morning," said De Luca, addressing the old woman, who looked at him with her mouth open. "I'm trying to find the porter."

Pugliese entered and pulled aside a curtain that separated the room from the rest of the apartment. A cabbage pot was boiling on a range.

"I don't know anything," said the old woman. "My husband's out and I don't know anything."

"But you know the gentleman upstairs, don't you?" De Luca asked. The old woman shrugged.

"I'm not the one who knows everybody," she said. "That's my husband."

"Well, to look at him he seemed like a nice person, that man," said Pugliese wheedlingly. The old woman turned toward Pugliese with a start, making the rosary beads tinkle.

"A nice person? With all the women visitors he received up there at all hours? Don't know much about people, do you?"

"What does receiving some nice girls mean nowadays . . ."

"These days there are no nice girls. It's the war's fault. Just this morning there were two of them here, one was that blonde, a pretty girl but crazy as a loon, and strange, a Count's daughter, my husband said . . . And the other one, a brunette with glasses, another strange one . . . But I don't know anything. Every now and again I see something from in here, because I'm old and I've got a pain in my legs that . . ."

"Fine," De Luca said brusquely, cutting the woman short, and behind his back Pugliese shook his head. "Besides the two ladies, did you see anyone else go up this morning?"

"No, my husband, maybe . . ."

"Okay, we get the idea. Where is your husband?"

"After the police arrived," she said pointing at Pugliese, "he went out on an errand." De Luca looked at Pugliese, who shrugged.

"He'll be back," he said.

"Let's hope so," said De Luca. He turned and started towards the door, but the old woman stopped him, beginning to speak again.

"A nice person!" she said bitterly. "With all the misery that's around these days, bread that's up to fifteen lire a kilo, when you can find it that is, and him throwing money away! Who can say where it come from . . . and he was also getting about with the Germans!"

"Germans?" asked Pugliese. He glanced at De Luca, who was looking at the old woman.

"That's right. My husband told me, because I'm no expert when it comes to these things, but there was this soldier who'd visit, an officer, and he had red flashes on his collar, with those . . ." With a sharpened nail at the end of a thin finger she traced two parallel marks in the air and Pugliese turned aside with a grimace.

"That's done it," he said. "The SS."

"Even better," said De Luca. "At least we'll be through quickly. Tell me something else: did that gentleman have a maid? A servant?"

"Oh yes. Assuntina." De Luca allowed himself the shadow of a tired smile. "From down South, she was, an evacuee. She was permanent there with him, though if you ask me, things like that are not right . . . But she left three days ago."

De Luca turned once more and this time nobody stopped him. He left the porter's room, and Pugliese hopped along behind him to the front steps. Outside a GNR patrol was stopping people, their machine guns in full view. A man in civilian clothes who was checking papers greeted De Luca, who didn't respond.

"What now?" Pugliese asked, putting on his hat. He seemed shorter with the hat.

"We have to report back to the chief of police. We tell them that a questionable character, a Party member, a friend of the SS as well as of Count Tedesco's daughter—whose father, by the way, is no less than a member of the Republic's diplomatic corps and a personal friend of Marshall Graziani—has been killed and castrated by who knows who, with a weapon that has gone missing. If only it had been the poor, jealous maid; she has been missing for three days, no less, from a home in which the beds were made this morning. We know this thanks to the information given us by a porter who this morning most helpfully decided to run an errand, despite the police and a dead body upstairs. What do you think the Chief will say?"

"What will the Chief say?" Pugliese repeated with a wry smile.

"What I'm about to say now." De Luca pulled his badge out from inside his trench coat and opened it before a militiaman who was heading towards them with a menacing look. "Out of my fucking way, son," he said. "This here is none of your business. Just forget it."

CHAPTER TWO

"Forget it? You're crazy, De Luca, what are you saying?" The Chief got up out of the armchair and came out from behind his desk, planting himself in front of De Luca, who was sitting uncomfortably in a wooden chair as stiff as an accused man, his arms folded across his chest, looking at the floor.

"Listen, there's been a crime, a serious crime at that, and we can't simply forget about it. You went to great lengths to get yourself transferred to the police, and now you come up with crap like this. It's not like you."

De Luca didn't say anything, keeping his eyes fixed on the floor. Behind him, slouched in an armchair, with one leg over an armrest, lazily dangling a shiny boot, was Federale Vitali, Party Secretary, who watched him in silence, a tight smile on his thin lips.

The Chief went back behind his desk, but didn't sit; he remained standing, authoritative, hands in waistcoat pockets, at the top of the curve of his rotund belly, right beneath the pugnacious jaw of Il Duce hanging on the wall.

"If something is scaring you," he said paternally. "If someone is putting pressure on you, or seeking to prevent justice from coming out into the open, it is our duty to—"

"It is Il Duce's express will," Vitali said without getting up, "and ours, too, obviously, that the police carry out their duties without impediments, for those matters within their jurisdiction. Why, the police must arrest thieves and murderers so that the Italian people know that in fascist Italy, even in difficult times, the law is always the law! Over here things are not as they are in the South, where scum and Badoglians treat the law like their plaything . . . An important case like this must serve to show people that the police force is present and watchful!"

The Chief gestured with his hand, nodding solemnly, as if to say that those were his words. He sat in the armchair, which squeaked under his weight.

"Just to be clear," said De Luca. "What is it you want me to do?"

The Chief smiled. "You're one of the best police investigators around; you were before going to the Brigata Muti, and you are now. Investigate. Find the murderer."

"In complete confidence, of course . . ."

"On the contrary, Commissario." With a rustle of his black fascist uniform Vitali got up and stood behind De Luca, making his boots creak. "On the contrary: You will be furnished with generous space in the papers and all means will be at your disposal. Full support from the Party."

He too walked around the desk and stopped beside the Chief. He was a small, edgy-looking man, with raven hair that was swept back and plastered down with grease. De Luca looked at them at length, in silence, and then nodded.

"I understand," he said. "I find Rehinard's murderer. Then?"

"Then you arrest him. Handcuff him and take him to jail. Isn't this your job?"

"Even if it's a Count?"

"Even if it's a Count."

"Even if it's a German?"

Vitali grimaced, stretching his thin lips. "Of course, a German, no. But that is obvious."

"Obvious," echoed the Chief. "Good, that's enough chatter, go to work. You're on this case only; you'll be supplied with a car and all the men you want. The Federale has put the Milizia on hand for whatever help may be needed."

Vitali clicked his shiny new heels with a loud snap, bowing his head, and then tensed.

"Commissario De Luca," he cried. "Fascist Italy is watching you! Saluto al Duce!"

FROM *ZULU*

By Caryl Férey

Translated from the French
by Howard Curtis

The world capsized into the ocean of night and Brian Epkeen fell deep into an abyss, then woke with a start. The noise of the sliding door had made a kind of click in his head. The noise came from downstairs, not loud but perfectly audible. After a while it stopped.

Brian rolled over in bed, narrowly avoiding the head on the pillow next to his, and retreated to take stock. The birds were chattering beyond the bedroom window, curly red hair peeped out from beneath the sheets, and someone had just entered the house.

Brian reached for his revolver, but it wasn't on the desk. He saw the head turned away from him, the tousled hair, but no clothes on the floor. He slid out of the sheets without a sound, grabbed the .38 from under the bed, walked naked across the carpet to the door, and softly opened it.

He felt woozy, he still didn't know where his clothes were, but there was definitely someone downstairs. He could hear footsteps heading out of the living room. The person was rummaging in the hall now. He crept down the stairs, rubbing his eyes, which were taking their time to focus. When he got to the foot of the stairs, he flattened himself against the wall. The intruder hadn't had to climb over the railings to get in—the gate had been left open.

Now completely awake, Brian gripped the handle of his gun. He didn't know why he had left everything open, but he had a good idea—the redhead upstairs. In any case, the house was too big for him, it wasn't just a matter of the security system anymore. He advanced toward the hall, gripped by contradictory feelings. Silence seemed to have seeped into the walls of the house, the birdsong had stopped. Brian crept around the corner and stopped for a moment in surprise. There was the thief, rifling through the pockets of his jacket, which by some miracle was actually hanging on the coat stand.

The intruder had just found two hundred-rand bills in the wallet when he sensed a presence behind him.

"Drop the money," Brian said, in a hoarse voice.

Even though caught in the act, the other man didn't flinch. He was a young white, about twenty, dressed in the latest fashion—Gothic boots, baggy jeans, an extra-large T-shirt with a picture of a hardcore band on it—and with long light chestnut hair like his mother's.

"What are you doing here?" David retorted, staring at his father, the bills still clutched in his hand.

"I could ask you the same question," Brian said. "This is my house."

David did not reply. He put the wallet back in the jacket, but not the bills. There was no trace of remorse or shame on his cornfed Brad Pitt face. The prodigal son seemed to be in a hurry.

"Is this all you have?" he asked, indicating the bills.

"I stashed the rest in the Bahamas."

Brian hadn't moved, hoping that the revolver would hide his nudity, but David was looking with an air of disgust at his father's big dangling cock.

David was studying journalism. He smoked grass, was always broke, an idler. His mother's beloved son, their only son, their star, arrogant as could be and clever enough to have set up house at the home of his girlfriend's parents. He was a new-generation white who considered himself a leftist liberal, and not only spoke about the SAP[1] in insulting terms but called

[1] South African Police.

his father a fascist and a reactionary. It really hurt him to hear that, like a blow to the gut, but all the same, Brian loved his son—he'd been the same at his age.

This wasn't the first time David had come here to steal from him while he was asleep. The last time, he'd not only gone through his pockets but also the pockets of the girl who'd been sleeping upstairs.

"I need money," he said.

"You're twenty years old, look after yourself."

Brian tried to grab the bills, but David stuffed them in the extra-large pocket of his jeans and looked around for whatever else he could swipe.

"Did your mother send you?" Brian asked.

"You didn't pay her this month."

"It's only the second, damn it."

"It wouldn't make any difference if it was the tenth. How do you think she gets by?"

David had more than one insult in his armory. Brian grinned bitterly. He had borrowed money to keep the house, hoping that David would come and live here, with his girlfriend if he wanted, or his boyfriend, he really didn't care. But not only had his son not wanted to come, Ruby had continued to fill his head with lies.

"I hear your mother drives around in a BM coupé with that dentist of hers," he said. "She should be able to survive till the end of the month, don't you think?"

"What about me?"

"Your school fees, the two thousand rand I send you every month, isn't that enough?"

Behind his grunge rebel hair, David was sulking. "Marjorie's parents have thrown us out," he said.

Marjorie was his girlfriend, a Goth with piercings everywhere—he'd seen her seen once or twice coming out of David's school.

"I thought her parents really liked you."

"Not anymore."

"You could come and live here."

"Very funny."

"Why don't you go to your mother's?"

"She has her new life now, I don't want to piss her off. No, what we need is an apartment in town, not too far from the faculty. We'd like to rent in the Malayan quarter, but you have to pay the first two months in advance, then there's food, and bills."

"Don't forget taxis. Best way to get to the faculty, don't you think?"

"So what about it?" David said, impatiently.

Brian sighed again, touched by so much love.

It was then that David noticed the woman's dress hanging on the chair in the hall. "I see you're entertaining," he said. "Do you know this one's name?"

"Didn't have time to ask. Now get the hell out of here."

"And you, go wash your dick."

David brushed past him, walked across the living room without a word, and slammed the door, leaving a deafening silence in his wake.

Brian wondered how the little boy who used to run after penguins on the beach could have become this skinny stranger who acted like some kind of mother superior, and was cynical about everything. What saddened him wasn't so much the fact that he'd found him rifling his pockets while he was asleep as the way he had of leaving without a word, just giving him that horrible look, always the same one, a mixture of contempt and bitterness, as if he was seeing him for the last time. Brian put down the revolver he was still holding—it wasn't loaded anyway—saw his crumpled clothes on the kitchen table, the purple blouse on the floor, the matching bra, and went glumly back upstairs.

It was hot in the bedroom. The woman with the curly red hair was still lying on the bed, the sheets now down below her buttocks. They were diaphanous, curvy, as fine and soft as wax. Tracy, the barmaid from the Vera Cruz. A thirty-five-year-old redhead with bleached bunches he'd been seeing for a while, small but hot stuff.

Sensing his presence, Tracy opened her apple-green eyes, and smiled when she saw him. "Hi."

Her rumpled face still bore the marks of the pillow. He wanted to kiss her, to erase what had just happened.

"What time is it?" she asked, making no attempt to cover herself.

"I don't know. About eleven."

"Oh, no!" she simpered, as if they had only just fallen asleep.

Brian sat down next to her, with one leg still out of the bed. The confrontation with his son had laid him low, he felt like some kind of creature washed ashore, being pecked at by seagulls and crows.

"What's the matter?" she asked, stroking his thigh. "You seem worried."

"No, I'm fine."

"In that case, get back in bed. We have plenty of time, before we go to your friend Jim's."

"Who?"

Tracy's eyelids performed an arabesque. "Your friend. Jim. You told me we were going to spend Sunday by the sea. He gave you the keys to his villa."

Brian did a double take—oh, God, he really should stop using the famous Jim. The last time he'd raved about this so-called friend, it had been to invite a young woman lawyer to come and play golf in his private club in Betty's Bay. What on earth possessed him to talk about the guy? He must have a sick mind.

Tracy pulled back the sheets, revealing two creamy breasts,

which, if his memory served him well, were very sensitive. She smiled. "Come here, you."

Brian let himself be drawn in by what her fingers were doing. They stimulated each other's senses for a while, worked themselves up into a frenzy, both came, although not at the same time, exchanged a few exhausted caresses, and finished it all off with a kiss.

A few moments later he disappeared into the bathroom and took a shower, wondering what he could say to sweet-talk Tracy, then looked at his image in the mirror and decided not to bother.

Brian Epkeen had been handsome, but that was in the past. There had been too many fuck-ups, too many missed opportunities. Sometimes he hadn't given enough love, sometimes he'd loved too much, or else gotten it all wrong. For forty-three years he'd been scuttling about like a crab, sometimes wandering far off course, sometimes making sudden sideward leaps.

He grabbed an unironed shirt, which, in the mirror, vaguely reminded him of himself, put on a pair of black pants, and strolled across the bedroom. Tracy, still lying on the bed, was asking him to tell her more about their Sunday by the sea when Brian switched on his cell phone.

He had twelve messages.

*

Cape Town lay at the foot of Table Mountain, the magnificent massif that towered three thousand five hundred feet above the South Atlantic. The Mother City, it was called. Brian Epkeen lived in Somerset, a gay area full of trendy bars and clubs, some open to everyone, without restrictions. European colonists, Xhosa tribesmen, Indian and Malayan coolies—Cape Town had had a mixed population for centuries. It was the country's flagship city, a little New York by the sea, but also the place where Parliament was located, which meant that it was here that the apartheid policy was first applied. Brian knew the city by heart. It had both inspired strong emotions in him and just as often made him nauseous.

His great-great-grandfather had come here as a ragged, illiterate farmer who spoke the kind of degenerate Dutch that would become Afrikaans, believed in an eye for an eye, and wielded the Old Testament in one hand and a rifle in the other. He and the Boer pioneers with him had found a barren land peopled by Bushmen with prehistoric customs, nomads who couldn't tell the difference between a game animal and a domestic one, who pulled the legs off cows and ate them raw while they mooed to death, Bushmen they had driven out like wolves. The old man didn't spare anyone—if he had, there was a good chance his family would have been slaughtered. He refused to pay taxes to the English colonial governor who left them alone to face the hostile natives, clear the land and survive as best they could. The Afrikaners had never depended on anyone or anything. That was the blood that Brian had in his veins, the blood of dust and death—the blood of the bush.

Whether out of some ancestral memory, or some sense of being a dying race, the Boers were the eternal losers of history—following the war that took their name when British conquerors burned their houses and their land, twenty thousand of them, including women and children, had died of hunger and disease in the English concentration camps into which they had been herded—and the establishment of apartheid had been their greatest defeat[2].

In Brian's opinion, the reason his ancestors had established apartheid was because they were shit scared. Fear of the black man had taken over their bodies and minds with an animal

[2] The Natives' Land Act, granting 7.5 percent of the land to the native population, was the beginning of apartheid.

force that recalled the old reptilian fears—fear of the wolf, the lion, the eaters of white men. That wasn't the basis on which to build anything. Phobia of the other had destroyed their powers of reason, and although the end of the despised regime may have restored some dignity to the Afrikaners, fifteen years weren't enough to wipe out their contribution to history.

Brian drove past the quaint old buildings in the city center, then the colorful facades of the colonnaded houses on Long Street. The avenues were largely free of traffic, most people had gone to the beach. He climbed toward Lions Head, managing to get a little coolness by putting his hand through the open window—the air-conditioning in his Mercedes had long since given up the ghost. A collector's item, just like him—Tracy had said that, and he had taken it as a compliment. He wasn't thinking about her as he drove, or about the weekend with "Jim."

David's intrusion had left a bitter taste in his mouth. They had hardly spoken for six years, and when they had it had been so unpleasant it would have been better to keep quiet. Brian hoped that things would work out, but David and his mother still bore him a grudge. He had cheated on her—that was true—mostly with black women. Brian was faithful only to his beliefs, but when you came down to it, it was all his fault. Ruby had always been a tragic, deeply wounded fury, and he'd been a complete idiot—it was plain as could be that the woman was a force-ten storm warning. They had met at a Nine Inch Nails concert during a festival in support of the release of Mandela, and the way she had been exploding in the middle of that electronic din should have made him sensitive to the cyclones to come—a girl who bounced up and down to the riffs of Nine Inch Nails was obviously pure dynamite. Brian had fallen in love, an encounter of two parallel lines suddenly converging, a hot beam of love making straight for her crazy eyes.

In Constantia, Epkeen narrowly missed the colored with the

bandaged head zigzagging in the middle of the road, and stopped at the red light. The man, his shirt torn and blood-stained, walked on a little way, then collapsed, and lay there in the sun with his arms out. Other down-and-outs were sleeping it off on the sidewalks, too befuddled with alcohol to hold out their hands to the few passersby.

Brian turned at the corner of the avenue and took the M3 in the direction of Kirstenbosch.

Two police vehicles were blocking access to the Botanical Gardens. Brian saw the forensics van in the parking lot, Neuman's car parked close to the souvenir shops, and groups of tourists disconcerted by the irritability with which they were being turned away. The clouds were tumbling from the top of the mountain like frightened sheep. Brian showed his badge to the constable manning the barrier, passed under the arch of the big banana tree at the entrance, and, pursued by swarms of insects, followed the birdsong to the main path.

Kirstenbosch was a living museum, a multicolored tide of plants, trees, and flowers stretching to the foot of the mountain. On the English-style lawn, a pheasant flew off as he passed, making a mocking sound as it did so. Brian reached the acacia grove.

A little farther on, he saw His Majesty, his tall frame stooped beneath the branches, talking in a low voice with Tembo, the medical examiner. An old black in green overalls was standing behind them, cut in half by the shade and his overlarge cap. One lab team was taking prints from the ground, another had nearly finished taking photographs. Brian nodded to Tembo in his jazzy felt hat—he was just leaving—and the old man in his municipal overalls. Neuman was waiting for him before he himself left.

"You're not looking too good," he said when he saw him.

"In ten years, my friend, just you wait."

At that moment, Brian saw the body in the middle of the

flowers, and the front he had been keeping up since the minute he woke up this morning, already somewhat undermined, now crumbled a little more.

"It was this gentleman who found her this morning," Neuman said, indicating the gardener.

The old black said nothing. It was obvious he didn't want to be there. Brian bent over the irises, taking deep breaths to steady his nerves. The girl was lying on her back, but it was the sight of the head that made him recoil. You couldn't see her eyes, or her features. She'd been wiped off the map, and her tensed hands, which seemed to be reaching toward an attacker both unseen and omnipresent, made her look as if she was petrified with fear.

"The murder took place about two o'clock last night," Neuman said, in a mechanical voice. "The ground's dry, but the flowers are trampled and stained with blood. Probably the victim's. There are no bullet holes. All the blows are concentrated on the face and the top of the skull. Tembo thinks it was a hammer, or something similar."

Brian was looking at the white, blood-spattered thighs, the slightly plump legs—a girl David's age. Chasing away these visions of horror, he saw that she was naked under her dress.

"Rape?"

"Hard to say," Neuman replied. "We found her panties beside her, but the elastic is intact. We know she had sexual intercourse. What we still have to establish is if it was consensual or not."

Brian moved a finger over the girl's bare shoulder and lifted it to his lips. The skin had a slightly salty taste. He put on the latex gloves Neuman handed him, examined the victim's hands, her bizarrely retracted fingers—there was a little earth under the nails—and the marks on her arms: small grazes, in almost straight lines. The dress was torn in places, leaving big holes.

"Two fingers broken?"

"Yes, on the right hand. She must have been trying to defend herself."

Two male nurses were waiting on the path, their stretcher on the ground. Standing in the sun all this time was starting to get on their nerves. Brian straightened up, his legs like mercury.

"I wanted you to see her before they took her away," Neuman said.

"Thanks a lot. Do we know who she is?"

"We found a video club membership card in the pocket of her cardigan, registered to Judith Botha. A student. Dan's gone to check it out."

Dan Fletcher, their protégé.

The insects were buzzing under the acacias. Brian swayed for a moment to avoid them. Neuman's eyes were like two black suns—the sense of foreboding that had been with him since dawn hadn't left.

From *The Midnight Choir*
By Gene Kerrigan

GALWAY

It was just gone noon when Garda Joe Mills got out of the patrol car on Porter Street, looked up and saw the jumper sitting on the edge of the pub roof, his legs dangling over the side. Garda Declan Dockery was still behind the wheel, confirming to radio control that this was a live one. Looking up past the soles of the jumper's shoes, to the pale, bored face, Joe Mills was hoping the fool would get on with it.

If you're gonna jump, do it now.

Thing about people like that, they don't much care who they take with them. Mills had once worked with a garda named Walsh, from Carlow, who used to be stationed in Dublin. Went into the Liffey after a would-be suicide and the guy took him under, arms around his neck. Would have killed him if Walsh hadn't grabbed his balls until he'd let go.

The jumper was just sitting there, two storeys above the street, staring straight ahead. He looked maybe forty, give or take. The sleeveless top showing off his shoulders. Bulky but not fat. He paid no heed to the arrival of the police or the attention of anyone below. To the left of the pub there was a bookie's, and a motor accessories shop to the right and beyond that a branch of a building society, all with a trickle of customers. Passers-by slowed and some stopped. An audience was building. As Mills watched, several pre-lunch drinkers came out of the pub to see what was going on. Two of them were still clutching their pints.

Mills waited for Dockery to finish talking into the radio. He wasn't going up on that roof alone.

Thing like this, edge of the roof, all it takes is he grabs hold of you at the last moment, your arm, maybe, or the front of your jacket—and your balance is gone. You reach for a hand-hold and you're too far out and all you get to do is scream on the way down.

You want to jump, go ahead. Leave me out of it.

A man in his fifties, pudgy, balding and pouting, button-holed Garda Mills. "I want him off there, right? And I want him arrested, O.K.?"

"And you are?"

"The manager. I want him dealt with. That kind of thing—this is a respectable pub, right?"

Mills saw that the jumper was shifting around. Maybe his arse was itchy, maybe he was working on a decision.

"Oh, I dunno," Mills said. "Thing like this, you could have a lot of people dropping around to see where it happened. Tourists, like. Can't be bad for business."

The manager looked at Mills, like he was considering if there might be something in that.

"I want him shifted, right?"

Dockery was standing at Mills's shoulder. "Ambulance on the way. They're looking for a shrink who can make it here pronto. Meantime—"

Mills was thinking, traffic in this town, by the time a shrink gets here it'll all be over.

One way or the other.

Dockery was looking at the assembled gawkers. "I reckon the most important thing is we cordon off down here. We don't want him coming down on top of someone."

Mills nodded. That sounded like the sensible thing to do. Best of all, it was ground-level work. Dockery was already moving towards the onlookers when one of the drinkers said, "Oh, no."

Mills looked up. The jumper was standing.

Shit.

Mills said, "We can't wait for the shrink."

Dockery said, "Wait a minute—there's—"

Mills was moving towards the door of the pub. He took the manager by the elbow. "How do I get up there?"

"Joe—" Dockery was making an awkward gesture, caught between following Mills and moving the gawkers out of harm's way.

The manager, grumbling all the way, took Mills up to the top floor, where a storeroom led to an exit onto the roof.

Mills was trying to remember a lecture he'd attended a couple of years back. How to approach a possible suicide.

Reluctantly.

The roof was flat tarmac, with razor-wire barriers jutting out at a forty-five-degree angle on each side. The storeroom took up a quarter of the roof space at the back and there was a two-foot-high parapet at the front. Near the centre of the roof a green plastic garden chair lay on its side, next to a stack of broken window boxes and a couple of empty old Guinness crates. At the front of the building the jumper was standing on the parapet, arms down by his sides. Mills moved towards him at an angle, stepping sideways, keeping his distance. He wasn't going close enough to be pulled over, and he didn't want to startle the man.

From up here, the jumper looked like he was in his early thirties. Denim jeans, trainers and the dark blue sleeveless top. Well built, serious shoulders and biceps that didn't come from casual exercise.

Weights, probably steroids too.

What to say?

Mills couldn't remember much from the lecture, but he knew that there was no point arguing with a jumper. Logic didn't work. Whatever it was had got him out here it'd be so big in his mind that there wouldn't be room in there for reasoning.

Get him talking. Draw him out. Make a connection. That's a start.

Maybe ask him if he's got kids?

No.

Could be domestic.

Mention kids and I might step on something that stokes him up.

It was mid-April and Mills could feel the winter overhang in the breeze.

Down there, touch of spring. Notice the wind up here.

"Cold out here. In that top."

Fuck's sake.

The weather.

The jumper stared straight ahead.

"You a regular in this pub?"

Nothing.

Should have asked the manager.

"You want to tell me your name?"

Nothing.

"Don't know about you, but I'm nervous up here."

Mills was trying to remember something that the lecturer had said. About how, more often than not, the subject is using the threat of suicide as a cry for help. Offer a way out, show them that you care.

O.K., fella, I hear you.

Well done.

Point made. Help on the way. Quit while you're ahead.

Say hello to the men in white coats and they'll give you all the little pills in the world and by tomorrow you won't remember what was bothering you.

Or what planet you're on.

The jumper turned his head just enough so that he was looking Garda Joe Mills in the eye.

Jesus.

The man's blank icy stare was unmistakable evidence that this was no cry for help.

There's something mad in there.

The jumper held Joe Mills's gaze as he turned completely around until his back was to the street and he was facing the garda.

Ah, fuck.

His arms still down by his sides, his heels an inch from the edge of the parapet, his expression vacant, the jumper stared at Joe Mills.

Now, he falls backwards, staring at me until he goes out of sight and the next thing I hear is the gawkers screaming and then the wet crunching sound that I'll be hearing in nightmares for years to come.

"Look, fella. Whatever it is—I mean, what you need to think about, give it time—"

Stupid.

Arguing—he can't—

The jumper stepped lightly off the parapet onto the roof. He stood there, chin up, his bulky tensed arms several inches out from his sides. After a few seconds he flexed his jaw in a way that made the tendons in his neck stand out. Then he took an audible breath and began to walk past Garda Mills. He was moving towards the storeroom and the door down from the roof.

"Hey, hold on—"

Mills reached out to grab an arm and the man threw a punch. Mills felt like his nose had taken a thump from a hammer. The jumper was turning sideways, instinctively positioning himself to block a return blow, but through the pain Mills was very deliberately suppressing his own urge to lash back. He was already ducking to the left, one hand snapping onto the jumper's right wrist, then he was twisting the man's hand and moving around him, keeping the arm taut, twisting it and pushing and the jumper made a *Hwwaawwh!* sound and Mills was standing behind him. The man was bent forward ninety degrees, immobilised by Mills's grip on his hand and his rigid arm.

Mills hooked a foot around the man's leg so that when he pushed the jumper forward he tripped and went down, his arm held rigid all the way. The anguished sound the prisoner made seemed to come in equal measure from the pain and from the realisation that he had no control over what was happening.

Mills could hear footsteps behind him and then Dockery was reaching down and seconds later the man was cuffed, belly down on the roof.

Mills felt the elation rush from somewhere in his chest, spreading out right to the tips of his fingers, blanking out even the pain in his nose.

Did it!

Situation defused.

Every move totally ace.

If Dockery hadn't been there, Mills might have given a whoop.

He wants to go off a roof, there's always tomorrow, and to hell with him, but for now—

Gotcha!

Mills took a deep breath and Dockery said, "Jesus, look at that." He was pointing down at the man's cuffed hands.

Mills could see dark reddish-black stains on both hands, across the palms, in between the fingers. The dried blood was caked thick around the man's fingernails.

Dockery turned the prisoner over. There were darker stains on the dark blue top. There were also dark streaks down near the bottom of his jeans. The man lay there, quiet, like the fight had drained out of him in that short frantic struggle.

Dockery was looking at Mills. "He's not hurt?"

Mills shook his head. "Can't be his blood. And it's not recent."

That much blood—someone was carrying a hell of a wound.

Mills looked at his own hands, where he'd gripped the nutcase. He saw a smear that might have come from the stains on the man's hand. He rubbed his hand on his trouser leg.

He bent and looked at the man's trainers. There were dark reddish marks ingrained in the pattern of the sole of one of them.

Might be, or maybe not.

Mills knelt, levered off both the man's shoes and held them by the laces.

Dockery said, "What's your name?"

The man ignored the question. Lying on his back, cold eyes watching Joe Mills straighten up, there was a twist to one side of his mouth as though his face couldn't decide whether to scowl or smirk.

They got him to his feet and hustled him towards the roof doorway, from which the pub manager was emerging. As they went past, the manager poked a finger at the prisoner. "You're barred, you are. You hear me? Barred."

DUBLIN

On the way out to the Hapgood place Detective Garda Rose Cheney pointed out the house that had sold for eight million. "Around here, the houses go for—what—pushing a million, and that's for your basic nothing special. One and three-quarters if they have a view of the sea, three if they back onto the beach. Any size on them at all and you're into four or five mil."

Detective Inspector Harry Synnott wanted to tell her that he didn't much care about Dublin property prices, but this was the second time he'd worked with Garda Cheney and she was a bit of a yapper. If it wasn't property prices it'd be something else.

Cheney steered around a gradual bend and slowed down. "That's it on the left, third one in from the end."

It was a tall handsome house, glimpsed through a curtain of

trees. Victorian? Georgian, maybe—Harry Synnott didn't know one period from another. Anything old that looked like a bit of thought had gone into it he reckoned was probably Victorian. Or Georgian. If not Edwardian.

"*Eight million?*"

"Eight-point-three."

"Jesus."

Rose Cheney snickered. "Couple of rich men got a hard-on for the same sea view. Nice aspect, mind you. Worth maybe three million, tops. Not that I'd pay that for it. Even if I had three million. But the way the market is, I mean, place like that'd run to three million, there or thereabouts. But you know how it is, bulls in heat, and the bidding went up to eight-three before one of them threw his hat at it."

Nice aspect.

Synnott wasn't sure what a nice aspect was, but it was apparently worth a rake of money. One minute the country hasn't an arse in its trousers, next minute the millionaires are scrapping over who gets to pay over the odds for a nice aspect. There were some who claimed the prosperity was down to EU handouts, others said it had more to do with Yank investment. There was a widely proclaimed belief among the business classes that they'd discovered within themselves some long-hidden spark of entrepreneurial genius. Whatever it was, the country had been a decade in love with its own prosperity and everyone agreed that even though the boom years were over there was no going back.

We might, Synnott thought, be card-carrying members of the new global order, but we're still committing the same old crimes. The working day had started for Synnott when he met Detective Garda Rose Cheney at the Sexual Assault Unit of the Rotunda Hospital.

Cheney had already interviewed the alleged victim and was waiting outside her room while a nurse did whatever it is nurses do when they usher visitors from a hospital room.

"Name is Teresa Hunt. Just turned twenty, doing Arts at Trinity. Family's from Dalkey, she has a flat in town. The doctor confirms she had recent intercourse, swabbed for sperm, so we might get something. She's not physically damaged, apart from minor bruising around her arms and thighs."

"Who's the man?"

Cheney opened her notebook. "Alleged assailant, Max Hapgood. They were an item sometime last year, met again at a party a couple of weeks back. He called her a few days ago. Had a date last evening, ended up back at her flat, and you know how that one goes."

Synnott shrugged. "It'll be a she-says-he-says. How'd she strike you?"

"See what you think yourself."

Teresa Hunt turned out to be a thin, wispy young woman who looked Synnott in the eye and said, "I want that bastard arrested."

Synnott's nod might have meant anything.

"You had a date," Cheney said.

"I told you."

"Tell the Inspector."

The woman looked slightly resentful that telling her story once hadn't set the seal on the matter. She turned to Synnott. "We had a date."

"And?"

"We had a meal, a drink. It was good to see him again. I assumed maybe he was having second thoughts, you know." She made a small dismissive gesture with one hand, like she was brushing away threads of illusion.

"You and he have a history."

"It didn't last long—it was no big deal."

Synnott heard something in her tone—perhaps it was a bigger deal for Teresa Hunt than she wanted to remember.

Cheney said, "The relationship was sexual?"

Teresa nodded. "We saw each other on and off, with other people—it's a small scene—but it tapered off. Then, when he rang, I assumed—"

Synnott sat back, let Cheney ask the questions. She did so gently but without skirting anything. There was no sign of the yapper now, just a capable police officer ticking off the boxes. Age of the alleged assailant? About the same as that of the alleged victim. He too was a TCD student. Business studies. Where it happened—in the woman's flat, on the floor of the living room. What time—between eleven and midnight. Yes, she asked him in for a coffee. Yes, there was affection, just a kiss or two. Yes, she consented to that. No, she didn't agree to have sex. Not in words, gestures or actions. Cheney took her through all the signals that meant one thing but might have seemed to mean another.

"It wasn't that kind of evening. It was hello-again, and that was that. I was happy to leave it that way. Then it was like he'd gone through all the right motions and it was time for the payoff. He pushed me down—"

Again, Cheney methodically took Teresa through the moves that might have been taken for a signal of some kind. No, she'd just had a couple of drinks. Same for him, two pints. Yes, she had made it clear that she was saying no. Yes, she'd said the word. Again and again. Yes, she'd struggled. No, he hadn't threatened to assault her.

"I scratched him, his face, but he just laughed. He's tall, strong." Quietly, with a twist of the lips. "Rugby type."

"Afterwards, what happened?"

"It was like, he was just normal, smiling, trying to make conversation."

"You?"

"I went into my bedroom. Then he left, called in through the door, said goodbye."

"This was about, what—"

"We got home, I don't know, maybe midnight, I wasn't keeping track. He didn't stay long."

"His car, yours?"

"Taxi."

A couple of questions later, Teresa went silent, her eyes and lips compressed. When it came, her voice was a hiss. "He—just—I was *nothing*. Like it was something he wanted to prove he could get away with." She wiped her eyes with the back of one hand.

Cheney said to Harry Synnott, "I'll make the call." They'd need Hapgood's address, and they'd have to request a preliminary check to see if he had a record.

Synnott shook his head. "I'll do it. You stay with Teresa."

When Garda Rose Cheney came out of the hospital room, Inspector Synnott was at the nurses' station, his mobile to his ear while he scribbled in the notebook that was open on the desk in front of him. Two nurses were chatting loudly about something that had happened the night before in A&E, while a doctor stood by a computer workstation, bent over the screen, clicking a mouse.

When Synnott finished he and Cheney found a corner where they couldn't be overheard.

Synnott said, "No previous. Hapgood has an address in Castlepoint." He nodded towards Teresa Hunt's room. "What do you think?"

"We may have a problem."

"I thought she was impressive enough."

"After you'd gone I went back over how they came to arrange the date. Seems Teresa wrote to him, got his address from the phone book. Suggested they get together."

"What she said was that *he* rang *her* for a date."

"He did, but before that—she bumped into him at a party, a week later she sent him a note. He rang her the next day."

Synnott said, "Well."

Both Synnott and Cheney knew that rape cases can fall one way or the other when they come down to a conflict of evidence. This one could be made to look like a young woman refusing to let go of a passing romance, pursuing the man to a sexual reprise. Depending on the sequence of events, the elements were there to create a defence that when Hapgood walked away, having no interest in Teresa Hunt beyond a quick roll, she made a revenge accusation. With a case that weak it wasn't in anyone's interest to let it go as far as a charge.

Cheney said, "It doesn't mean she's lying about the rape."

"No, but if Hapgood's kept the note and if what she wrote is in any way juicy, that's it as far as the DPP's office is concerned."

"It's still her word against his."

"The state doesn't like being a loser. If the odds don't stack up the DPP will pass."

The Hapgood place in Castlepoint was way over on the Southside, on the coast. They drove there in Garda Cheney's Astra. It was a big house, set well back, but it was on the wrong side of the road. No beach access. Rose Cheney parked the car and said, "What do you reckon? Two million, tops?"

Synnott said, "Depends on the aspect."

3.

The American tourist put his MasterCard back in his wallet and took the money out of the ATM. As he slipped the notes into the wallet he heard his girlfriend make a frightened noise. He turned around. Kathy was pale and rigid, staring off to one side. The mugger was four or five feet away, a woman in—what?—her mid-thirties. Thin legs in faded blue jeans, a shabby red jacket too big for her frame. Her long hair was blonde, tied back untidily, she was blinking a lot and holding one arm stiffly down by her side. What the American tourist mostly saw was the syringe she was holding in that hand, the blood inside it a darker shade than the red of her jacket.

"Give it," she said.

"Take it easy, now—"

Neary's pub, where the tourist and his girlfriend had had drinks the previous night, was across the street. Down to the right were a couple of restaurants, customers sitting at the windows, people coming out of a fish shop across the road, others crossing towards the specialist kitchen shop, no one paying attention. It was pushing lunchtime and fifty feet behind the mugger, at the end of the side street, the usual throng of Grafton Street shoppers flowed by unheeding.

The woman stuck her chin out. "You want the HIV?"

"Just—"

"Just fuck off—give me the money—"

"Thomas—" The American tourist's girlfriend was holding out a hand to him. "Do what—"

The mugger said, "*She* can have it—" She waved the syringe towards the girlfriend.

The man made calming gestures, both hands patting an invisible horizontal surface in front of him. Thomas Lott, the manager of an upmarket sandwich shop in Philadelphia, had been almost a week in Dublin, Kathy's home town, her first trip home in four years. Thomas had long ago decided that the sensible thing to do if ever he was mugged would be to hand over whatever money he had, and that was what he intended doing. He just wanted things to calm down.

No room in Kathy's parents' house, so they'd stayed in the Westbury. After six days in the city Thomas found Dublin bigger and less folksy than he'd expected. Lots of sandwich bars and coffee shops, just like Philly. Lots of tall shiny glass buildings to provide the sandwich bars with their customers, just like

Philly. Just as many shopping malls as Philly, just as many overpriced restaurants and just as many dead-eyed shoppers. And now, it seemed, just as many muggers.

The mugger's voice had a hysterical edge when she hissed, "Give me the fucking *money*!"

Across the street an elderly woman and her middle-aged daughter, both raven-haired and wearing fur collars and dark glasses, were staring at the mugger.

"Sure, O.K.—"

Thomas Lott felt the strap of his black leather shoulder bag slip down his right arm and his left hand automatically reached up to catch it. He saw the mugger's mouth widen, her eyes move this way and that and he knew that she thought he was trying something and he thought for a fraction of a second that he should say *No, it just slipped!* But there wasn't time, so he caught the sliding strap in his right hand and he swung the bag hard. As soon as he did he felt a dart of horror at his own foolishness—then he saw the bag connect, and the syringe was knocked sideways, flying out of the mugger's hand, and he felt a giddy rush of triumph.

Backing away, the mugger screamed a string of obscenities. Thomas Lott started towards her, but she was already turning, bent and running.

"*Thomas!*"

Lott gave up the notion of following the mugger. He roared, "Stop her!" but she was already about to turn the corner into Grafton Street, slipping into the tide of unheeding pedestrians.

"Thomas."

When he turned back, Kathy was standing very still, breathing heavily, like she was trying not to scream. Thomas Lott moved towards his girlfriend and he was within three feet of her before he saw the syringe, ugly against her dazzling white skirt, sticking up out of the front of her thigh at a forty-five-degree angle.

FROM *A DARK REDEMPTION*

By Stav Sherev

1

The coffee machine wasn't working. It burbled, hissed and spluttered to a stop. Jack Carrigan stared at it in disbelief. He'd bought it only three months ago and it was supposed to last a lifetime. He turned it on and off, jiggled and gently shook it, and when that didn't work he hit it twice with the side of his fist. The machine coughed, hummed, and then, miraculously, started pouring what looked like a passable cup of espresso.

The sound of the coffee slowly oozing through the steel and silver pipes always made him feel better. He began to notice the morning, the thin streamers of sunlight leaking through the gap in the curtains he'd never got round to fixing, the sound of cars being put through their morning shuffles, coughs of cold engine and shriek of gears, the doors of houses closing, the patter of tiny feet on the pavement, the clatter of human voices arising from the early-morning air.

The machine groaned once and stopped. He reached for the cup, the smell making his mouth tingle, and was just about to take his first sip when the phone rang.

He staggered over to the table, his fingers brushing lightly over Louise's photo, picked up the receiver and held his breath.

Carrigan walked through the park trying to shake off the previous night. He'd arrived back from the coast late, scraped the mud from David's grave off his shoes and fell heavily onto the sofa where he'd awoken crumpled and cramped this morning. It had been a last-minute decision; he'd be down there with Ben in a couple of weeks but something yesterday had called him, a pulse beating behind his blood.

He spent a few minutes staring at the trees, soaking in the heat, trying to ignore what lay waiting for him on the other side of the fence. Late September in Hyde Park was his favourite season, the grass still scorched by summer's sun, the trees heavy, the first leaves fluttering down to the waiting ground. He closed his eyes and Louise's face rose out of the dark, this park her favourite place, holding hands in snowstorms, watching kids playing by the pond, both of them thinking this life would last for ever.

Carrigan exited the park and walked on the road to avoid the clots of tourists emerging from Queensway station. He watched them huddling in tight packs, wearing the same clothes, staring up at the same things. He envied them their innocence, seeing London for the first time, a city with such history yet without personal ghosts. When you'd lived here all your life you stopped seeing the city and saw only the footsteps you'd carved through it, a palimpsest traced in alleyways and shop windows, bus stations and bends of the river.

He reached the building and looked around for Detective Superintendent Karlson, whose call had interrupted his morning coffee, but he was nowhere to be seen. He took out his phone and made sure he had the right address. Two PCs had been called to a flat in King's Court earlier. When they saw what they were dealing with they immediately called the Criminal Investigation Department.

Carrigan looked up at the towering facade and pressed the porter's buzzer. He knew the building well. They received a call every week about something, mainly waste-of-time stuff, noise complaints, funny smells, burglar alarms going off for no explicable reason in the middle of the night, but, like any building with over five hundred residents, it had its share of domestic abuse, suicide and small-time drug dealing. He tried the buzzer again. He could hear voices crackling faintly through the intercom, conversations in languages he didn't recognise, floating in and out of hearing, criss-crossing each other until they dissolved into static and white noise.

A woman with a pram was wrestling the door from inside. Carrigan held it open for her and, as she thanked him, slipped past into the marbled lobby, its cool mirrored surfaces and swirling carpets making him feel instantly dizzy. He knocked on the door to the porter's booth but there was no answer. He peered through the frosted glass, squinting his headache away, and saw the slumped shape of a man inside. This time he gave it his four-in-the-morning police knock.

When the door opened the stink hit him like a fist. Body odour, cigarettes and despair. The porter was a small withered man with three-day stubble and eyes that looked as if they never stopped crying. His face twitched intermittently, revealing dark gums and missing teeth as he struggled to pull himself back together. Jack knew exactly how he felt.

'Detective Inspector Carrigan.' He showed the man his warrant card but the porter only nodded, not looking at it or at him, and shuffled back into his room, collapsing onto a chair whose stuffing poked out like mad-professor hair.

The porter's cubicle looked as if it had once been a luggage locker. There were no windows, no room for anything but a table, a chair and four small TV monitors with a constantly running video feed of the building's entrance. The porter was breathing heavily, lost in the screen, watching the unpeopled doorway with such riveting poise it could have been the last minutes of a cup final he was witnessing.

Carrigan shuffled a few steps forward, bending his head to avoid the low ceiling. He took small, shallow gulps of the stale air. 'You keep spare keys to individual flats?'

The porter barely acknowledged him, a faint turn of the head, nothing more. He eventually looked up from the screen and scratched his stubble. 'Not no more. Used to be everyone left them with me, but things change.' He didn't elaborate how.

'Flat 87's the one directly above 67, right?'

The porter nodded. 'I thought you guys were in 67?'

'We are,' Carrigan replied tersely, wishing he'd had time to get breakfast. 'Do you have keys for flat 87 or not?'

The porter opened a drawer and pulled out an old ledger. He rapidly flicked through the pages. Sweat poured down his face as he squinted at the shaky handwriting. He ran one yellowed finger down a list of numbers, then stopped. 'Uh-huh. Flat 87. No spare.' He zoned out in front of the screen again. Carrigan craned his neck but there was only the image of the front door, fish-eyed, black and white, empty. He thanked the man, found out when his shift ended, and left the sweatbox of an office.

He saw the two constables nervously chatting outside the door to 67. The look in their eyes told him this wasn't just a prank, something they could all laugh about on their way back to the station. He nodded, walked past them and knocked on the door. He waited as a series of locks tumbled and unclenched until the door finally opened and an old woman stared at him as if she'd never seen a man before. It took him a few seconds to realise she was or had been a nun, the habit faded and worn, the crucifix dangling like a medallion from her thin wattled neck.

'I'm Detective Inspector Carrigan.' He showed her his warrant card. The old nun didn't acknowledge, just turned and walked back into her flat.

He was never surprised at how people lived and yet he was always surprised. Fifteen years on the job, how many flats, houses, mansions had he been into? How many lives marked out by the geography of walls? He told all his young constables that the key to a person was in how they lived their lives—study their surroundings, how they chose to arrange themselves in this world—you'll learn much more from that than from listening to them talk or staring deeply into their eyes.

He walked through the small hallway and into the living room. The furniture was mismatched, as if collected over time from disparate sources. Chipped and cracked paint everywhere. Pieces of drawers and light fittings missing, replaced if at all by masking tape. The carpet was worn and thin, showing through to the floorboards. Stains described maps across the floor like countries never visited, dark and sticky spots where tea or ketchup or custard had landed. The old nun coughed, hacking into her hand. She lit a cigarette, the smell instantly filling the room.

The mantelpiece and bookshelves held no books, only a staggering variety of porcelain dogs. Carrigan stepped closer and saw they were all West Highland terriers, produced in a variety of finishes and styles. A few looked almost real while others were the product of some kind of artistic myopia, resembling sheep or clouds more than they did dogs.

But it was the two pieces at the far end of the mantelpiece he couldn't keep his eyes off. It was these two that the old lady was silently pointing to with the end of her cigarette. These dogs weren't white like the rest. They were red. A crimson caul covered their bodies.

The old nun was gesturing at them, speechless, as if such a thing had no referent in language. Her eyes had receded deep into their sockets and when she pulled on the cigarette she looked like a Halloween skull. Carrigan inched forward. He looked at the dogs and then he looked up.

A patch of red, in the shape of a teardrop, was slowly spreading from one corner of the ceiling. The constables followed his gaze and, as they watched, a single red drop fell, exploding against the white mantelpiece like an exotic flower.

2

Carrigan walked up the stairs to the next landing, his heart sinking, his feet dragging behind him. He couldn't see where the hallway ended. The mangy carpet disappeared into a funnel of darkness a few flats down. It reminded him of those long nightmare corridors in *The Shining,* a film he wished he'd never seen; its images promiscuous and relentless long after the watching was over.

The hallway was lit from above by twitching fluorescents recessed under a metal grille that rained down the light in black spears against the walls and carpet. The air seemed packed tighter here than on the floor below, filled with heavy, textured smells, the various scents commingling and forming new alliances in the corridor. All around buzzed the noise and hum of lives lived behind closed doors. Muffled announcers on blaring TV sets, broken conversations, pounding drum and bass. The rotten reek of cooked cabbage and garlic. Arguments and shouting. A faint whiff of weed.

He heard the two constables come up behind him, their faces pale with what they'd seen and what they were about to see. He stopped in front of number 87 and knocked. Two old ladies wrapped in thick muslin that made them look mummified walked past, their eyes lingering on Carrigan, unspoken suspicion in every muscle twitch. He ignored them, knocked once more, then got to his knees.

There was no letter box, but he could see a half-inch gap between the front door and the hallway's filthy carpet. He pressed his face against the floor, feeling the sticky shag-pile grab at his beard, but he couldn't see any light coming from inside the flat. He moved, pressing his face closer, took a deep breath and immediately started coughing. He took one more to be sure, then got up, brushed the dirt off his clothes, and called it in.

He sent the constables back downstairs and waited for the

scene of crime officers to arrive. He spent the time watching the flow of bodies in and out of flats, a constant shuffle of lives enacted in this dim and dank hallway. He knocked on adjacent doors. There was no answer from the flats either side of 87. He knocked on the flat directly opposite. The door opened and an unshaven man with a cigarette that seemed moulded to his lips looked at Carrigan and said, 'Huh?'

Carrigan showed him his warrant card, asked if he knew who lived opposite. The man wouldn't make eye contact with him. Somewhere inside the flat Carrigan heard a woman shouting in Greek, Romanian, he didn't know, the man's eyes narrowing as if each word were a splinter driven into his flesh. 'No police,' he said. 'I done nothing wrong.'

Carrigan wedged his foot in the door as the old man tried to close it. The old man looked up at him, a rabbity fear in his eyes. 'I'm not interested in you.' Carrigan pointed to the flat across the hall. 'I want to know who lives there.'

The man looked down at his slippers, torn grey things exposing yellowed and cracked toenails. He shook his head but the action seemed to be commenting on something bigger than Carrigan's question. 'I seen nothing and I don't want to see nothing.'

This time Carrigan let him shut the door. People in these blocks never heard or saw anything; he knew that from experience. It wasn't that they had anything to hide, not like trying to canvass witnesses in a hostile estate, but in the countries they'd fled from a knock on the door could mean imprisonment, torture and often worse. How were they to know that police all over the world weren't the same?

The SOCOs and DS Karlson arrived a few minutes later. They suited up in the stairwell and gave Carrigan his oversuit, latex gloves, and foot protectors. The starchy chemical smell filled his nostrils as he unsnapped the gloves and slipped them on.

'Any idea what's in there?' Karlson was filling the sign-in sheets, smiling that thin begrudging smile of his. He'd never liked Carrigan, couldn't understand why someone with a university degree would want to be a policeman. Didn't like the fact that Carrigan hated sports, wouldn't drink the station's Nescafé and rarely joined the others for after-work drinks down the pub.

'We'll see when we break down the door, won't we?'

Carrigan moved back as the two constables took hold of the ram. The door was old, had been painted over so many times it cracked in two like a rotten fingernail. The stench hit them immediately.

'Jesus Christ.' One of the constables, Carrigan always forgot his name, pedalled back so quickly he ran right into Carrigan, his body warm and taut like a greyhound's.

Carrigan stepped past him, taking a deep breath. His nostrils filled with a metallic sweetness and he wished he was in the corridor again with the garlic and cabbage, anything but this.

It was a studio flat. Small and self-contained. A narrow hallway, kitchen to the left and bathroom to the right. The bedroom/living room stretched out in front of them. At the far end a small window opened out onto a rectangle of sun and trees. Carrigan focused on the leaves, golden brown already, as they swayed and trembled on the branches. Then he looked back towards the bed.

Her arms were tied to the ends of the headboard. Her arms looked as if they'd been stretched beyond their capacity, the skin tight against the bone. Translucent plastic ties snagged her wrists to the brass. He could smell the dark heated mulch of blood, ammonia and sweat. He tried breathing through his mouth as he stepped closer.

He could hear the constables cursing behind him, Karlson taking deep swallows of air, the clutter and clump of the SOCOs setting up their equipment, but they all seemed as far away as the detonation of trance music that was coming from an upstairs flat.

He stared at the girl as flashbulbs popped and burst. Her body was sporadically revealed by the light then disappeared back into darkness.

Her nightdress had been cut down the middle so that it hung on either side of her torso like a pair of flimsy wings. The knife had gone deep into her chest, a dark red line running from navel to ribs. He stared at the wide canyon carved into her stomach, the dark brown shadows and glints of white poking from within. He felt last night's dream rise in his throat and he swallowed hard to keep it down, taking short breaths, keeping his feet evenly spaced. He saw Jennings, one of his young detective constables, catch a glimpse of the bed, then rush straight to the bathroom. Outside he could hear doors being slammed, the shuffle of feet and ongoing lives, but in here there was only the stillness of death.

He didn't want to look at her face so he looked at her legs. It was almost worse. Small puncture wounds ran like bird tracks criss-crossing her skin. He leant closer. Too small to have been made by a knife or blade, grouped in pairs. He moved back and saw that they continued up the torso and along the undersides of her arms. Small pointed punctures, black with blood, evenly spaced, the flesh around them mottled, torn and weeping. They looked like animal bites, he thought with a shudder.

'Christ, what the . . . ?' Karlson stared down at the open cavity of her chest, the perforation of her limbs, her cracked front tooth.

Carrigan said nothing, headed for the window, took a deep breath as he watched the laundry flutter in the courtyard. He could see people going about their daily chores oblivious and unconcerned. He turned back, finally ready to look at her face. He stood next to Karlson, smelling the man's sweat and fear, the reek covering his own. He tried not to look at her chest, the gaping hole, white shards of bone poking out like stalagmites, but the wound had its own terrible gravity. He heard Karlson curse under his breath and turn away.

Behind him, a scene-of-crime officer was setting up his video camera, his colleagues drawing out strange containers of powder and unguent, miraculous dispatches from the frontiers of science. One man was unpeeling a roll of sticky tape, the horrible screaming sound filling the room as he cut it into strips in preparation to 'tape' the body; a slow and painstaking job intended to capture any rogue hairs or fibres caught on the skin. The man looked up at Carrigan and shrugged. The SOCOs wanted them out, they had work to do, evidence to collect. They didn't even see the girl, she was only a surface from which information could be gathered, conclusions drawn.

Carrigan bent down again, ignoring them. He put his mouth to the dead girl's ear. They heard him whisper something to her but not what he said. They looked at each other uncomfortably. This was hard enough without the senior investigating officer talking to the dead, but Karlson and Jennings only shrugged; they'd learned to ignore the idiosyncrasies of their DI. Carrigan surveyed the girl's body once more then leant back in and froze.

'Karlson, over here,' he said in a dry, raspy voice. He stood over the body as the sergeant looked at the cavity in her chest.

'What?' Karlson said. 'I can't see anything.'

'Exactly,' Carrigan replied, pointing through the ribs at the empty space underneath. 'It's not there.'

Karlson stared at him, confused, then looked back down at the body.

'Her heart,' Carrigan said. 'It's gone.'

FROM *THE CROCODILE*

By Maurizio de Giovanni

Hush a bye baby,
Oh, I'll give you a star.
Sleep pretty baby,
It's the brightest by far.
Hush a bye hush a bye,
Now do you want the moon?
For the sweet love of God,
Go to sleep, darling girl.

CHAPTER 1

Death comes in on track 3 at 8:14 in the morning, running seven minutes late.

He blends in with the commuters, jostled by backpacks and briefcases, suitcases wheeled and otherwise, none of them able to sense the icy chill of his breath.

Death walks hesitantly, protecting himself from the haste of others. Now he stands in the vast concourse of the train station, surrounded by shouting children and the smell of thawing pastries. He takes a look around, wipes away a tear from behind the left lens of his eyeglasses with a quick motion, whereupon his handkerchief returns to its place in the breast pocket of his jacket.

He identifies the exit, from the noise and flow of the crowd, amidst all the brand new shops. He no longer recognizes the place: everything is different after all these years. He's planned out everything to the smallest detail. This search for the exit is going to be the one and only moment of hesitation.

No one notices him. A young man leans against a column smoking a cigarette; he runs his gaze over and past him as if he were transparent. It's a clinical look he's just given him: nothing worth stealing, his down-at-the-heel shoes and unfashionable suit speaking as eloquently as the transition lenses and the dark necktie. The young man's eyes slide past him, coming to a halt on the half-open handbag dangling from the shoulder of a woman gesticulating frantically as she talks into her cell phone. No one else sees Death as he moves warily through the atrium of the train station.

Now he's outdoors. Humidity, the smell of exhaust. It has just stopped raining, and the sidewalk is slippery with oozing muck. A shaft of sunlight breaks through, and Death squints in the sudden glare, wiping away another tear. He looks around and spots the taxi stand. He trudges along, dragging his feet.

He climbs into a battered vehicle. The interior stinks of stale smoke, the seat sags listlessly. He murmurs an address to the driver, who repeats it loudly in confirmation as he jerks the car into motion and pulls into the stream of traffic without a glance behind him. No one honks their horn.

Death has come to town.

CHAPTER 2

Sergeant Luciano Giuffrè rubbed his face with both hands, pushing his glasses onto his forehead as he massages his eyes.

"Signora, this is getting us nowhere. We have to come to some kind of an understanding. We can't have you coming in here and wasting our time. We have urgent work to do. All right now, would you tell me exactly what happened?"

The woman compressed her lips, shooting a sidelong glance at the neighboring desk.

"Commissario, don't talk so loud. I don't want *him* hearing things that are none of his business."

Giuffrè raised both arms in a gesture of helplessness:

"Listen lady, for the last time: I'm not the Commissario. I'm just a lowly sergeant with the hard luck to be assigned to this desk, where I'm in charge of taking complaints. And *he* isn't eavesdropping on things that are none of his business. He's Lieutenant Lojacono, and he has the same job I do. But, as you can see, he's been luckier than me. For some reason, in fact, no one seems to want to file their complaints with *him*."

The man sitting at the other desk showed no sign of having heard Giuffrè's tirade. He kept his eyes on the computer screen and his hand on the mouse; but he seemed to be lost in other thoughts.

The woman, a middle-aged working class matron with a small purse clutched in her plump hands, made a great show of ignoring him.

"What can I tell you, customers always go to the salesmen they trust."

"What do you mean by talking about salesmen, Signora? Now you're going to make me lose my temper! Really, how dare you? This is a police station: show some respect! Customers, salesmen, where do you think you are, a butcher shop? Now, either you tell me immediately, in the next two minutes, exactly what happened, or I'll have the guard usher you out of here. Ready?"

The woman blinked her eyes rapidly:

"Forgive me, Commissario. I must just be a little tense this morning. What you need to know is that the woman downstairs has started taking in cats again. And now she has three, you understand? Three."

Giuffrè sat staring at her:

"Okay, and what are we supposed to do about it?"

The woman leaned forward and muttered, under her breath:

"These cats meow."

"Oh Jesus, of course they meow, they're cats. There's no law against that."

"Then you're determined not to understand: those cats meow and they stink. I leaned over the balcony and I said to her, perfectly sweetly, I said: listen, you miserable loser, will you get it through your thick skull once and for all that you need to move out of this building, you and your filthy creatures?"

Giuffrè shook his head:

"Damn, it's a good thing you said it sweetly. And what did she say to you?"

The woman straightened her back on the chair, to underscore the depth of her indignation:

"She told me to go fuck myself."

Giuffrè nodded, agreeing with the spirit if not the letter of the cat-owner's sentiments.

"Well?"

The woman opened her piggy eyes wide:

"Well, now I want to file a criminal complaint, Commissario: you need to haul her in here and slap her in a cell, her and the cats she keeps. I want to report her for aggravated instigation to self-fucking."

Giuffrè didn't know whether to laugh or cry:

"Signora, there are no cells in here and I'm not the Commissario. And as far as I know, there's no law on the books against instigating someone to go fuck themselves. Moreover, it strikes me that you called the woman downstairs a 'miserable loser' first, am I right? Listen to me, why don't you just go home, try to keep your temper under wraps, and remember that a couple of cats never hurt anybody, and they even catch mice. Go on, now. Please stop wasting our time."

The woman got to her feet, rigid with disgust:

"So that's what we get for paying our taxes, is it? I always say to my husband, he shouldn't declare half of the merchandise he sells. Have a nice day."

And she stormed out. Giuffrè took off his thick-lensed glasses and smacked them down on his desktop.

"I have to ask myself what I ever did wrong in a previous life to deserve this job. How on earth, in a city where we have to go out every morning and count the dead bodies in the streets, could a woman like that decide to come into the police station to file a complaint against another woman who told her to go fuck himself, and with every right to do so, if I might add? Does such a thing strike you as conceivable?"

The occupant of the neighboring desk took his eyes off the monitor for a brief moment. His face had vaguely oriental features, dark, almond-shaped eyes, high cheekbones, shapely, fleshy lips. Tousled, unkempt locks of hair dangling over his forehead. He was a little over forty, but sharp creases at the sides of his mouth and eyes spoke of far older sorrows and joys.

"Oh come on, Giuffrè. That's just part of the nonsense. You need to have something to do to make the time go by in here, don't you?"

The sergeant snapped his glasses back onto the bridge of his nose, feigning astonishment. He was a very expressive little man, who seemed to amplify every word he said through mimicry, as if the person listening were deaf.

"Oh, and what do we have here? Has Lieutenant Lojacono woken up from his beauty sleep? What would you like now, a cup of coffee and a pastry? Or would you rather I bring you your morning newspaper, so you can read up on what the nation did while you were slumbering?"

Lojacono smiled with just half of his mouth:

"I can't help it if everyone who comes in here gives me a passing glance and then makes a beeline for your desk. You heard the fat lady, didn't you? The customers develop a certain loyalty to their favorite salesmen."

Giuffrè drew himself up to his full five foot five inches.

"You do know that you're a passenger in the same leaky boat as me, don't you? Or do you think you're just passing through here? You know what everyone else calls this office? They call it the Cottolengo. Just like the hospital in Turin, the one where they keep the seriously retarded and handicapped. So what do you think, that they're singling me out?"

Lojacono shrugged.

"Well, what the hell do I care? They can call this shithole whatever they like. I'm more disgusted by it than they ever will be."

He turned back to his monitor, where there was a time and a date, right under the game of cards that he incessantly played against the computer. April tenth, two thousand twelve. Ten months, and a few days. For the past ten months, and a few days, he'd been sitting there. In hell.

From *Summertime, All the Cats Are Bored*

By Philippe Georget

Translated from the French
by Steven Rendall

Chapter 1

Robert got up at 4 A.M. As he had every day for the past forty years.

For him, it was neither he chose or was forced to do. That's just how it was. It didn't matter to him whether they were on daylight saving time or not: a four A.M. he woke up and immediately slipped out of bed.

He poured himself a cup of cold coffee. Added a drop of milk. Then he set the crossword puzzle aside so he could put his cup on the little table.

All his life, Robert had worked as a tool and die maker for a firm that manufactured agricultural machinery near Gien, in the Loiret region of France. He got to work a 4:30 on the dot and he had never been even a minute late. Well-regarded, valued by his superiors, not unionized, and polite. A model worker. Took a degree in economics as he approached the age of fifty-five.

He sat down on the narrow bench and drank the bitter, cold coffee, grimacing with distaste. He could have warmed it up, but he couldn't be bothered. In any case, he wasn't allowed to put sugar in it, so he might as well swallow it as fast as he could. At one point he'd tried drinking tea but had found the punishment more severe.

Although he had stopped going to work, Robert had not been able to change his internal clock. It drove Solange, his wife, crazy that he woke so early in the morning. So at the beginning of his involuntary retirement, he'd tried to stay in bed. To sleep in, at least until six o'clock. But he tossed and turned, wrapping himself in the sheets, so that his wife finally told him he could get up as soon as he woke. And then she had gone away. In a few months. Bone cancer.

Robert poured the dregs of his coffee in the sink and rinsed his cup. The water pump was humming in its cabinet under the bench. He put the cup in the drain rack and went out the trailer.

It was the middle of June, and "The Oleanders" campground in Argelès was still almost empty. A few retirees like Robert and a handful of foreign tourists. The Dutch always got there first, then the Germans. Robert went directly to the toilets. The day before, he had used the second stall from the left. Today, it would be the third. It was Wednesday.

He urinated slowly and voluptuously in a clean basin. A sweet odor of lavender filled the shack. That was what he had liked right away about "The Oleanders": the toilets were immaculate. They were cleaned regularly, and especially one last time late in the evening. Robert appreciated not having his nostrils brutally attacked first thing in the morning by the odors of the other campers' piss and shit.

He enjoyed it right down to the last drop that he let fall against the smooth and still clean side of the urinal. Once he had gone outside, he looked at his watch. 4:19. He washed his hands, as he had the day before, at the nineteenth sink in an endless row. Then he wiped his hands on his pants. He was ready for his daily walk. He foresaw that it would be the most difficult of his life. The white gravel of the lane that ran down the middle of the campground crunched under the leather soles of his sandals. Usually he liked this delicate little sound, but this morning he paid no attention to it.

Robert and Solange had discovered "The Oleanders" in

1976. Earlier, they had camped by the side of the road, or even simply slept in their old Diane. But after Paul, their son, was born, they wanted more comfortable arrangements. Then there had been Gérard and then Florence. The children had made friends in the campground. They were happy to see them again every summer. Robert and Solange had also formed habits. The parents of their children's pals had become their friends and vacations passed pleasantly, with games of pétanque, barbecues, and marathon card-playing tournaments.

Robert stopped by his trailer to be sure that he had locked the door. A mania of his. While his wife was alive, he'd controlled himself. But Solange was no longer there.

He turned the handle. The door resisted. It was locked. Obviously. Robert was proud of their campsite. The best set-up in the whole campground. There were two awnings that connected the trailer with a wooden deck next to a stone barbecue that he had built himself in 1995. The year he was dismissed. The whole thing was enclosed by a wooden fence on which a dozen flower pots hung. Before, it was Solange who took care of them. The first summer after she died, the pots had remained empty. Then Robert had picked up the torch. He liked putting flowers on the fence more than putting them on a grave.

Exposed to the sun and salt air, the green paint on the wooden posts was beginning to peel off. He'd planned to repaint them. He doubted that he could do it this summer.

The site was rented by the year. At the beginning of his retirement, they lived almost seven months a year at Argelès. Now the summer season exhausted him. He was sixty-five years old, and he felt tired. He would have preferred to spend the summer along the Loire River, but that was the only time when his children and grandchildren could come to see him. He crossed the campground, walking slowly and silently.

A ray of light was coming through the crack under the door

of a neighboring trailer that was registered in Germany. It belonged to a couple in the sixties. He was tall and fairly bald. She was petite, heavy, and had a permanent. They had argued loudly as they maneuvered the trailer into its spot. At first, Robert had laughed at them. Then he had felt very strange. He missed arguments since he had been living alone.

Just next door to the Germans, there was neither sound nor light in the tent occupied by the young Dutch woman.

Robert arrived at the little door that opened on the beach. It was closed but he had the key. Charles and Andrée, the managers of the campground, knew his early morning habits, and had long ago given him a key. Over time, they'd gotten used to each other. Robert sometimes gave them a hand doing maintenance work during the off season. A little job here and there. A sink to unstop, a part of the lawn that needed reseeding, a barbecue to be repaired. He liked doing that kind of thing, and in his trailer he didn't have much to do. Robert and Charles chatted as they worked, that occupied their minds. And then, contrary to what is often said, men are more likely to talk openly around a faucet to be changed than over a glass of anisette. Charles was the only one to whom Robert had been able to confide his distress when Solange died. One time he had even gone so far as to shed tears.

He started down the path that crossed the Mas Larrieu nature preserve. The birds, indifferent to his torments, were chirping their eternal hymn to life. Under their songs, the hoarse voice of the sea could already be heard.

The sea breeze was slowly rising, bringing in its nets a wild aroma of iodine and faraway places. The path led prudently between two wooden posts that were supposed to hold back the sand and channel the tourists. On both sides, flourishing prickly pears were vigorously growing their Mickey Mouse ears.

As he approached the beach, it became more difficult to walk, and Robert's feet sunk into the sand. The retiree started walking as close as possible to the fence in order to put his feet on the meager tufts of grass. Near a thicket of reeds, he hesitated. Then he decided to walk down to the sea first.

A few dozen yards more, and then he came out on the beach. The wind grew stronger, the aromas more intense. The surf was high this morning. On the horizon, the sky was already clearing. Life would go on. Imperturbable.

Robert walked as far as the changing line of the waves. He contemplated the somber mass of the sea and the white line of its crests. No sea would ever again carry his body, he told himself sadly. An immense loneliness invaded him. A total despair. His knees bent under the burden and forced him to suddenly sit down on the damp sand.

How he would have liked to turn the clock back a few hours. Yes, only a few hours . . .

Thoughts struck his mind without ever sticking. A wild sea-swell washing over the rocks. Solange, Florence . . . the only women in his life. Fragmentary memories of happy vacations surged up and were immediately wiped away by images of fury and blood. The storm was raging in his skull. He knew that it would stop only on the day of his death. As soon as possible . . .

He remained prostrated for endless minutes. When he raised his head, a red line was cutting across the horizon. The sun would soon be up. The first children were running on the beach, laughter, life . . . With difficulty, he decided to go back.

He planned to go back to bed. To pull the covers over his head like a kid. Childhood was so far away, and he felt so old. People say that someday we fall back into childhood. If only that were true. To rediscover the joy and innocence just before dying . . .

But the hour of freedom had not tolled for him.

Back in front of the thicket of reeds, he imagined he heard a slipping sound. A strange noise. He cautiously moved forward through the tall grass, following a trail of broken stems. And it was there, in a minuscule clearing made by the mortal struggle of two bodies, that he found the bloody corpse of the young Dutch woman.

FROM *THREE, IMPERFECT NUMBER*
By Patrizia Rinaldi

Translated from the Italian
by Antony Shugaar

PROLOGUE

Gennaro Mangiavento, stage name Jerry Vialdi, pulls past a line of tour buses along the Via Guglielmo Marconi. He parks his Napoli sky-blue Fiat 500 and blesses it for its compact size:

"At last, I can do without the Porsche Carrera. Now I'm finally my true self."

He looks at the people who have just stepped off the tour buses. The women are tricked out in evening gowns at five o'clock in the afternoon, sequins glittering against sweat-sodden makeup.

"Look at these rubes, here at this hour. They can write articles about me in *The New York Times*, but the real money still comes from the usual crowd of ragtag losers. I flew all the way down to South America to bring back Sanjoval, with trumpet and all, but has it done me a bit of good? I promoted that minimal pussycat to the rank of poet with the aid of my beautiful voice and piano, and has it done me a bit of good? I've had women, men, and money by the shovelful, but has it done me a bit of good?"

Vialdi sits in his car and remembers.

"Right here is where I picked and chose among the rejected lyricists, because they treat me with respect inside the RAI building; they have no choice but to put on their smiles, and Zampani lets me use his studio which by now is practically mine, since he's never there. When they came to see me to be hired, they'd say: I'm Antonio D'Antonio and I'm a writer. I'm Mario Coppola and I'm an experimental author. I'm Ferdinando Colasunto and I'm a poet. I always only had one answer: I'm Jerry Vialdi and I'm a piece of bad news and let me tell you, before I count to five you'd better be the fuck out of here. What the hell! Then Pussycat Mignon showed up, a name I came up with personally, and short and rickety as she was, she opened her mouth and started to speak. She didn't say I'm a poet, I'm a writer, I'm experimentally good at this or that, instead she said *you are the voice that stirs desire*. That's what she said. And I took her on, because as far as ugly goes, she was ugly, but once she started talking I forgot all about that; if I could forget the fact while I was looking right at her, then Pussycat Mignon, without her face in front of their feet, could have satiated vast populations with her words. We'd sell them like hotcakes. The exact opposite of Rosina, who decided she was done with me last year, the fool. If Rosina wants to maintain her credibility, what she has to do is keep her mouth shut tight: short red hair she has, a flaming brushfire that only needs stirring up, along with first-class thighs and throat. I didn't want to take her on at first because I used to go out on the town, and even run to women, with her husband; I knew him well and it seemed wrong somehow. But then Rosina got my blood pumping and I decided to hire her anyway, because if there's one thing I like it's when one of God's creatures can stand up to me, or even lose control entirely. Rosina never stopped hating me, which is always worth something: when she meets me now her eyes light up, even worse than that brushfire, and one of these days she's going to run me down with the car I gave her. A completely different level of danger, far more ferocious, attaches to Mara, the druggist. Sometimes I make a date with her and then stand her up: Mara's thighs and legs frankly frighten me, inside her stockings she carries a violent madness.

She's particularly good at the work she does. One night, she saved me from an attack of vertigo. I called her and she came, and when I saw her standing there with the hypodermic needle in one hand, I thought to myself: here we go, this is where she kills me. Instead, she healed me. Not Julia, she's a flower, a blossoming rose, a new young delicate jasmine bud. Of course, there's some tarnish on her bloom, because she's seen more than a few seasons in her time. She never makes high-handed demands, she's happy to take what we are for what we are; she's a different breed of woman, she has held onto her soul. I don't know how she's done it. I couldn't say, but perhaps she alone can conjure my soul back into existence. In any case, the most womanly of them all is still Gigi, and when he gets his claws into me he never lets me go, he's never even heard of the word soul or anything remotely resembling it. When he came into this world all he brought with him was his flesh; the spirit of the world beyond is something they clipped away along with his umbilical cord. He's a stunningly handsome devil. Forget about brushfires, he's got an eternal flame burning inside his chest. He's an advocate of pure evil and bad weather, with a mouth spewing gold and sea salt."

Vialdi gets out of the car. The flashing headlights tell him that the antitheft system is doing its job.

A woman in her fifties with rhinestone-studded shoes walks up to him.

"You're so good-looking, Jerry, you want to sign my record?"

"What do you have here, Signora? Did you dismantle the brakes on that bus?"

"What a charmer you are. You just have to make the dedication out to Annina." You have to this, you have to that. Jerry Vialdi's whole life has been a race to escape from *what you have to* and *what I tell you to*, and still they catch up with him. Almost invariably.

"I don't do dedications."

Before turning to enter the RAI building in Fuorigrotta, the ex-wedding singer, and later in his career ex-neomelodic pop singer, and still later ex-folk and traditional singer, and even later still ex-Ariston singer, then ex-star of musicals, until he finally became a sensitive singer winning the acclaim of the most discerning critics, turns and speaks to the looming horizon of the Polytechnic:

"If I'm ever reborn, I'm going to become an engineer and to hell with music and these ragtag losers in evening dress."

At the front door, the security guard doesn't bother asking for his pass, instead asking for predictions on the championship match.

"How's it going to go, boss?"

"This year is the *year*, brother, but we can't say it and we can't even think it because that's terrible luck."

Jerry Vialdi leaves nothing to improvisation; he even rehearses his smiles in front of the mirror. In his dressing room he checks his image; he twists his head to one side, swings one hand up to cover his chest, spreads his fingers wide and presses them against his sternum, then smiles:

"You are," pause, "you are all my own warm heart of love."

The concert is a success; the sole annoyance is the excessive applause, distinctly not to his liking: he wants to include a few of the better numbers in his next live album. Well, they have technicians to take care of that.

In spite of all the depth of his musical erudition, he inevitably hits the high point of the evening with the same song: a crass little ditty featuring words of furtive sex in a car and the subsequent return home to his cuckolded wife. The phrase *Tu, solo tu, sei tu—you, only you, it's you*—of the refrain is the song's earworm.

"A genuine piece of crap. What came over Pussycat Mignon

when she wrote it? Who can say? But I surely never thought she could produce such a generous helping of tripe! She turned in the lyrics four years ago. Let's set it to some fast-paced tune, loaded with percussion and *blam-blam* guitar riffs, she said. I objected, it's just too gruesome, I told her. You'll make enough money to buy a penthouse with another penthouse on top of it, she told me. And she was right, when I moved in to the double-decker penthouse in Pozzuoli with a view of the water I nailed platinum honors to the walls, tributes to the worst song and the fraudulent confection of percussion and *blam-blam* guitar riffs. And as usual, the money came and quickly left. Money: it scampers off on quick little cat's feet, the elusive imp."

Jerry Vialdi strips off his basic black stage outfit and fine-tunes his street clothes of autumn-hued cashmere and precocious corduroy trousers. The end of any concert still pumps him up to a boastful pitch and he channels into a flood of beauty and rare courage.

He caresses his inside jacket pocket, whispers *for later* and takes a few cautious sips of the preview of death.

1.

Detective Arcangelo Liguori was experiencing a moment of pure grace.

Even the sheer absence of minor defects forced him to admit how lucky he was. Even the fact that he had turned fifty, and really, a little more than fifty, struck him as once again youthful and useful.

He told himself that perhaps it was all due to August in Sicily and in Ireland, the love affairs remembered and archived, the rediscovery of his body in a late-breaking recovery of various activities. Perhaps it was a reward for his ability to think quickly about situations that did not concern him and which therefore tickled his curiosity just enough. The void had filled up with lovely and chaotic dovetailing elements.

He was feeling good, and that made him dangerous, now that his improved mood could be turned to the pursuit that he found most congenial: spoiling the good mood of everyone else around him, first and foremost among their ranks Captain Martusciello.

In October, his burgeoning animal spirits hadn't declined by so much as a fluid ounce and so, the minute he got back from the police station of Fuorigrotta, he strode into the administrative offices of Pozzuoli and went in search of Martusciello.

Captain Vincenzo Martusciello had spent what little summer vacation police regulations afforded him at a cut-rate holiday resort, with his wife Santina, his daughter Giulia, and his granddaughter.

Him, of all people—a man who refused to set foot on Procida in August for fear of succumbing to his phobia of crowds—had sunk to the level of bartering his family's dignity for a miniclub. Upon contact with the place, the children had shown no obvious signs of fatal pathologies. Though it wasn't clear why.

At the discount beach club, the water was like prairieland, the sand belonged to lands that had never seen rain. The local sunshine had killed off any breezes and stowed them away in the dreary ice-cream receptacles.

After a while, Martusciello stopped thinking of himself as a husband, a father, and a grandfather, and had gained a new respect for certain land animals that were capable of reproducing without having to stick around afterwards.

The line for the swings had given him an indelible sense of melancholy and an uncomfortable realization: expectations for the future were deader than the still-born breezes.

During the time he spent at the enchanting Ghiglia Resort, which he mentally referred to as Fanghiglia Risorta—*bubbling ooze*, it meant—he had half-persuaded himself that at least getting back to work would be a pleasure. He even expected to enjoy the morning commute on the ancient subway line, a term that was laughably applied to decrepit junk train cars running on creaky old tracks.

But that's not the way it went.

The sticky brine of melancholy relentless boredom had remained stuck to his heart, under his feet, and in the usual stab of pain on the right side of his body.

Upon his return, another inconvenience was joined to the long list of tiresome issues. The police captain found himself spending a week in the Ultramarine medical clinic, covered by his health plan, for the removal of a bodily appendage that he preferred not to discuss.

Laziness had been October's response. Walking the streets until he was ankle-deep in them no longer warmed his heart. He felt no interest in human beings, animals, the streetscapes of alleys, lanes, and piazzas, that reasoning of emotion and logic that had always induced him to undertake depositions and interrogations with the eagerness of a marathon runner.

Indignation had gone to ground and, with it, the desire to stage and restage the experience of life, like a stubborn village mule that only follows the route that it knows and yearns for, however unfashionable it may be.

His wife Santina, who was visibly rejuvenating for reasons unknown, gazed at him with a consummate love that plucked at his nerves.

"So tonight, again, you're not working, you're not going out?"

"I'm not going out."

"Why not?"

"You've tormented me for most of a healthy lifetime with your *why aren't you staying in*'s and now you're starting on me with *why aren't you going out*?"

"Do as you think best."

As you think best. Sure. There was nothing he wanted, there was nothing that interested him. He just wanted to step out of the line for the swings.

Liguori made his way to Martusciello's office by a roundabout route through a series of corridors, in order to avoid running into PFC Peppino Carità, who had informed one and all that he preferred to be addressed as Giuseppe Càrita—literally and precisely, with the accent weirdly on the first *a* instead of the last. This new development seemed to date back to the diction and acting course that he had taken recently.

Martusciello pretended to talk into the bakelite telephone that had accompanied him in his migrations from one office to another.

Liguori made himself comfortable and conveyed, with hand gestures, that he really wasn't in a hurry. Then he gave the police captain one of his goofy half-smiles, which reckoned up the sum of annoyance added to mockery.

Martusciello jutted his chin in the direction of the telephone and waved his free hand in a loose circle in the air to say *this may go on for some time*. The detective spread out the other half of his smile to say *I'm in no hurry*, and then went over to the window and stood, looking out.

Even though it was nearly noon, the colors hadn't yet merged into the hot haze of muggy sunlight. The sea lay there, crystal clear, the tiny waves sweeping in toward the waterfront, topped with foamy white crests. Even at this distance, the dark blue was still blue, the white was still white. The ferry boats to the various islands boarded a few scattered foreign tourists. Liguori surveyed the improvised seamen's uniforms. He ran one hand over his linen shirt before sliding it into the pocket of his duck trousers, artfully wrinkled as they descended to meet the tops of his expensive leather shoes, which had cost as much as half of Giuseppe Càrita's monthly pay.

Martusciello broke off his phone conversation with a non-existent colleague.

"Ah, gallant cavalier, a pleasure to see you!"

"Oh, it's been such a long time since I've been addressed by one of my rightful titles!"

Crime Cities

Profiles of World Noir environs

**Population data is most recent available for each city.*

ALGIERS, Algeria

Pop.:	2,988,145
Murder rate:	0.5 per 100,000
Book:	Inspector Llob Series
Author:	Yasmina Khadra
Perfect Protagonist:	Inspector Llob

Alger la Blanche—"Algiers the White" in French, sits shimmering on the coast of the Mediterranean, as corrupt as it is beautiful. Inspector Llob knows the city well, sees its imperfections and feels its struggles. He knows where to look when something isn't right, and when the seaside streets of his city are just a bit too quiet.

ATHENS, Greece

Pop.:	3,737,550
Murder rate:	1.3 per 100,000
Book:	Costas Haritos Series
Author:	Petros Markaris
Perfect Protagonist:	Inspector Costas Haritos

Amid the marble ruins of Democracy's city, Inspector Costas Haritos follows the thread of corruption within the police department and the government of Athens, only to find himself amid an entirely new set of ruins. Haritos grapples with morality and truth just as the ancients of his city might have; Haritos, however, finds no easy answers.

AUCKLAND, New Zealand

Pop.:	1,377,200
Murder rate:	0.9 per 100,000
Book:	*Utu*
Author:	Caryl Férey
Perfect Protagonist:	Paul Osborne

Paul Osborne has washed up in Sydney and is spiraling out of control. His former boss from the Auckland City Police Department has tracked him down after Jack Fitzgerald, a ex-colleague and Osborne's only real friend, committed suicide in the middle of an investigation. Osborne has no interest in playing policeman any longer, but he returns for one reason only: he's sure that Jack Fitzgerald couldn't have killed himself.

BUENOS AIRES, Argentina

Pop.:	2,891,082
Murder rate:	4.6 per 100,000
Book:	*Mapuche*
Author:	Caryl Férey
Perfect Protagonist:	Ruben Calderón

Calderón's own personal tribulations mirror his country's troubled history. A former journalist, imprisoned for his opposition to the government following the 1976 coup, he has driven himself to near poverty by hiring himself out for pesos (and sometimes not even that) as a PI to the Mothers of the Plaza de Mayo, searching for any trace of *los desaparecidos* and their odious tormentors.

CAPE TOWN, South Africa

Pop.:	3,497,097
Murder rate:	41 per 100,000
Book:	*Zulu*
Author:	Caryl Férey
Perfect Protagonist:	Ali Neuman

As a child, Ali Neuman narrowly escaped murder by Inkatha, a militant political party at war with the African National Congress. His father and brother were not so lucky. Today, Neuman is chief of the homicide branch of the Cape Town Police Department, where he does battle with Africa's two scourges: violence and AIDS. When the corpses of two young women are found, his job gets ever harder.

DUBLIN, Ireland

Pop.:	1,045,769
Murder rate:	2 per 100,000
Book:	*The Rage*
Author:	Gene Kerrigan
Perfect Protagonist:	Vincent Naylor

Just released from jail, Vincent Naylor resumes doing what he does best: planning for a robbery. Bob Tidey, an honest policeman discouraged by his colleagues' dealings with criminals, is investigating the murder of a Dublin banker. A meeting with an old acquaintance will change the course of his investigation, and when a retired nun sees something she can't ignore, she makes a phone call that sets in motion a series of fateful events.

EDINBURGH, Scotland

Pop.:	448,624
Murder rate:	2.5 per 100,000
Book:	Inspector Rebus Novels
Author:	Ian Rankin
Perfect Protagonist:	Inspector Rebus

We're not the first to notice that Edinburgh is actually two cities at the same time. It's the new city and the old; it's rational, full of light one minute, dark and twisted the next; its pubs and alleyways are both havens from the pelting rain and perfect places to break the bridge of your nose on some bloke's forehead. It's no accident that Jekyll and Hyde creator R.L. Stevenson grew up here. And no accident that Inspector Rebus is its best-known contemporary protagonist.

FRANKFURT AM MAIN, Germany

Pop.:	691,518
Murder rate:	6.2 per 100,000
Book:	Kayankaya Series
Author:	Jakob Arjouni
Perfect Protagonist:	Kemal Kankaya

As the financial capital of Europe, Frankfurt an Main is a precarious locale. Private Investigator Kemal Kankaya—more interested in a strong ale than he is in making a strong case—soon learns that deceit and corruption are entirely bipartisan.

HAVANA, Cuba

Pop.:	2,135,498
Murder rate:	6 per 100,000 (Cuba)
Book:	The Four Seasons Series
Author:	Leonardo Padura
Perfect Protagonist:	Mario Conde

In Leonardo Padura's Havana, passion and peril go hand in hand. The crumbling façades of the city shield both from public view, and Mario Conde must balance the demands of a crooked bureaucracy and the facts of daily life in Old Havana.

KIEV, Ukraine

Pop.:	2,797,553
Murder rate:	4.2 per 100,000
Book:	*Death and the Penguin*; *Penguin Lost*
Author:	Andrey Kurkov
Perfect Protagonist:	Viktor Zolotaryov

Chaotic, complicated, paranoid, surreal, violent and corrupt are all adjectives that could be applied both to Viktor Zolotaryov, struggling writer and hero of Kurkov's Penguin books, and to the city where he lives, post-Communist Kiev.

LONDON, England

Pop.:	8,174,100
Murder rate:	1.4 per 100,000
Book:	*A Dark Redemption*
Author:	Stav Sherez
Perfect Protagonist:	Jack Carrigan

Once a promising young musician, Jack Carrigan is now an inspector with the Metropolitan Police—a loner, unpopular with his colleagues because he is an expert at being the first detective at a crime scene to ensure that he will run the investigation. Now, the murder of a college student finds him caught between his obligation to follow the evidence wherever it leads and his superiors' concern for their jobs.

MARSEILLES, France

Pop.:	878,902
Murder rate:	Unavailable
Book:	*Marseilles Trilogy*
Author:	Jean-Claude Izzo
Perfect Protagonist:	Fabio Montale

Ex-cop, loner, and would-be bon vivant barely has time to shake off his latest hangover before the violence of Marseilles comes knocking at his door. Like a woman he can't leave, like a strong liquor he can't refuse, time and time again the ancient city lures Montale back into its violent embrace.

MELBOURNE, Australia

Pop.:	4,170,000
Murder rate:	0.57 per 100,000
Book:	*The Midnight Promise*
Author:	Zane Lovitt
Perfect Protagonist:	John Dorn

John Dorn works out of a tiny room in Melbourne's Chinatown. His only real friend is Dimitri, a Greek lawyer. His clients tend to belong to the huddled masses recently arrived on Australian shores. Dorn is a classic gumshoe with a drinking problem, a failed marriage behind him, and a good heart. This is crime fiction as a kind of sociological or urban tourism, from cramped flats in Coburg to nouveau-riche palaces in Sandringham, from encounters with depraved teenagers in Ferntree Gully and dimwitted crooks in Highpoint (aka "Knife-point") Dorn inhabits a modern Melbourne seething with tensions, but also vibrant and rich in urban lore.

MEXICO CITY, Mexico

Pop.:	20,450,000
Murder rate:	8.4 per 100,000
Book:	Héctor Belascoarán Shayne Novels
Author:	Paco Ignacio Taibo
Perfect Protagonist:	Héctor Belascoarán Shayne

One-eyed anarchist and independent investigator Héctor Belascoarán Shayne has a habit of finding himself neck-deep in more than one case at a time. He navigates the shadier side of a contemporary Mexico

City, rife with *narcotraficante* and suspicious deaths, taking what comes with a cigarette in one hand and a Coca-Cola in the other.

NAIROBI, Kenya

Pop.:	3,138,295
Murder rate:	4 per 100,000
Book:	*Nairobi Heat*
Author:	Mukoma Wa Ngugi
Perfect Protagonist:	Detective Ishmael

Detective Ishmael Fofona's encounter with Nairobi, a city still reeling from the genocide in neighboring Rwanda, a city where cops are trigger happy and oil rich oligarchs rule the roost, is a highly charged meeting of two worlds. Fofona is both insider and outsider and thus provides a fascinating portrait of the city.

NAPLES, Italy

Pop.:	959,574
Murder rate:	Unavailable
Book:	Commissario Ricciardi Series
Author:	Maurizio De Giovanni
Perfect Protagonist:	Commissario Ricciardi

A bitter wind stalks the city streets of Naples, and murder lies at its chilled heart. Commissario Ricciardi investigates the many murders in his seaside *città*, but he, too, carries a secret. He has become one of the most acute and successful homicide detectives in the Naples police force, but this may be a gift as well as a curse.

PADUA, Italy

Pop.:	213,623
Murder rate:	Unavailable
Book:	*The Goodbye Kiss, At the End of a Dull Day*
Author:	Massimo Carlotto
Perfect Protagonist:	Giorgio Pellegrini

Giorgio Pellegrini is a wanted man. To avoid prison, he sells out old friends, turns his back on his former principles, and cuts deals with crooked cops. He's getting too old for it, he knows, and in what may be the oldest city in Italy, how far is he willing to go to protect himself, and the life he used to live?

PALERMO, Sicily

Pop.:	653,522
Murder rate:	Unavailable
Book:	Inspector Montalbano Novels
Author:	Andrea Camilleri
Perfect Protagonist:	Inspector Montalbano

Inspector Salvo Montalbano has a passion for crime-solving, one that sends him far and wide chasing the details of one case after another, searching for justice and truth. At times listless, always nonconformist, Montalbano gets to the bottom of things even in spite of himself.

PARIS, France

Pop.:	2,234,105
Murder rate:	1.6 per 100,000
Book:	*The Prone Gunman*
Author:	Jean-Patrick Manchette
Perfect Protagonist:	Martin Terrier

Martin Terrier wants out of his mercenary life. He plans to settle down and marry his high school sweetheart—after just one more job. Assuming the shooting position once again, Terrier reveals a Paris not often seen, one with fewer illusions.

YSTAD, Sweden

Pop.:	18,350
Murder rate:	1 per 100,000 (Sweden)
Book:	Kurt Wallender Novels
Author:	Henning Mankell
Perfect Protagonist:	Kurt Wallender

The town of Ystad is a seaport, historically places where iniquity and illegality were concentrated. The town recently launched an Iphone application to guide visitors through Kurt Wallander's hometown. If that isn't the supreme example between fictional setting and its real life inspiration we don't know what is.

NOTES ON CONTRIBUTORS

Carl Bromley is the editorial director of Nation Books.

Andrea Camilleri is a Sicilian writer, best known for his serial character, Inspector Montalbano. In 2001, he was named a Grand Officer in the Order of Merit of the Italian Republic for his contribution to Italian letters.

Massimo Carlotto is one of the best-known crime writers in Europe. In addition to the many titles in his extremely popular Alligator series, and his stand-alone noir novels, he is also the author of *The Fugitive*, in which he tells the story of his arrest and trial for a crime he didn't commit, and his subsequent years on the run.

Caryl Férey is a French author. *Zulu*, his first novel to be published in English, was the winner of the Nouvel Obs Crime Fiction and Quais du Polar Readers Prizes. In 2008, it was awarded the French Grand Prix for Best Crime Novel. It is soon to be made into a film starring Orlando Bloom and Forest Whitaker.

Sandro Ferri is the editorial director and co-founder of Europa Editions, and the publisher and co-founder of Edizioni E/O in Italy.

Philippe Georget was born in Épinay-sur-Seine in 1962. He works as a TV news anchorman for France-3. He lives in Perpignan. His debut novel *Summertime All the Cats Are Bored* won the SNCF Crime Fiction Prize and the City of Lens First Crime Novel Prize.

Maurizio de Giovanni lives and works in Naples. His books have been translated into French, Spanish, German, and English.

As **Jean-Claude Izzo** was dying in January 2000, bookstores in his native Marseilles filled their shop windows with editions of his books in silent tribute to this unique man, who, in his profound humanity, his lust for life, and his many contradictions, embodied the soul of his native city. Marseilles repaid his love, providing him with the rich human dramas that he transformed into a fistful of extraordinary novels.

Tobias Jones, a former editorial assistant at the *LRB*, is the author of the bestselling *The Dark Heart of Italy*.

Gene Kerrigan is a Dublin writer. He was named Journalist of the Year in 1985 and 1990, and is the author of *The Midnight Choir*, *Little Criminals*, and *The Rage*, which won the 2012 Crime Writers Association Gold Dagger Award.

Dana Kletter is a musician and writer born in Baltimore and raised in New York. She was the lead singer of the punk band blackgirls, and the alternative rock group Dish. Her articles and reviews have appeared in *The Independent Weekly*, *San Francisco Chronicle*, and the *Boston Phoenix.* In 2010 she was awarded a Stegner Fellowship at Stanford University. She is currently at work on a novel-in-progress.

Carlo Lucarelli is one of Italy's most acclaimed and successful crime writers. He was born in Parma in 1960. His publishing debut came with the extremely successful De Luca Trilogy in 1990, and he has since published over a dozen novels and collections of stories. He conducts the program "Blue Night" on Italian network television. Among his many awards are the Scerbanenco Prize for *Via delle Oche*.

Michael Reynolds is an author, translator, and the Editor in chief of Europa Editions. He lives in New York.

Patrizia Rinaldi lives and works in Naples, where she was born in 1960. She is the author of numerous works of crime fiction published in Italy. *Three, Imperfect Number* is her first work to appear in English.

Stav Sherez is the author of *The Devil's Playground,* shortlisted for the Crime Writers Association Dagger Award, and *The Black*

Monastery. He spent five years as a music journalist, mainly for the cult music magazine *Comes with a Smile*. He has also written for the *Daily Telegraph*. He lives in London.

Benjamin Tammuz was born in Russia in 1919 and immigrated to Palestine with his family at the age of five. He was a sculptor as well as a diplomat, a writer, and, for many years, literary editor of the newspaper *Ha'aretz*. His numerous novels and short stories have been widely translated from the Hebrew and have been awarded an array of literary prizes. He died in 1989.

Charles Taylor is a writer living in Brooklyn, New York.

Valla Vakili is the CEO and co-founder of Small Demons. Prior to Small Demons he held several positions at Yahoo!, most recently VP Product for the Entertainment Group in Los Angeles.